From Here

Daniel Kramb

LONELY COOT

London

Published by the Lonely Coot

Copyright © 2012 by Daniel Kramb

Lonely Coot

London

lonelycoot.tumblr.com

ISBN: 978-0-9571925-0-8

First published in 2012

For my parents,
with love

One
Climate Change

"I mean, is there anything you regret?"

"No."

"Well, there you go."

Sometimes I lie because I have to; sometimes it just happens. Which one was this?

I nod.

My cutlery is silent in its end-of-meal position. What is it in these eyes that makes me talk so freely? So uninhibited?

What is it in this smile that stops me from looking away?

"Anyway – that was then, and this is now."

"Rest assured, you're not the first one who has ever reached this junction."

Junction – not a bad expression for the point I've reached. The point I shouldn't have mentioned.

"I'm just saying that I preferred the road."

"I figured that, yes."

"Anyway."

"Anyway."

The problem isn't that I don't want to talk to him about it; the problem is that I don't mind.

I crossed streets, borders and oceans for him, showed him my shower in a kitchen and the ramshackle bunk bed of my attic room. I let him in on my time in an old church, and the creepy few weeks I spent living in a former hospital.

I told him about the water-related development work, and the job as a theatre clerk, the coordination of a large-scale art project that fell through in the end, and the translation work that followed me wherever I went.

I couldn't help it. I painted the romantic picture of myself sitting next to my packed suitcase, my head turned towards yet another new destination, my eyes sternly ahead – always. For ten years, I was like that. For ten years, I was happy.

"It's amazing to hear all this. My life really seems boring in comparison."

I don't answer.

I took him through all my cities – all eight of them – and he loved it. I could tell.

And yet, every time I go through the list for someone now, it seems, a little more meaning is being sucked out of it. More and more, my cities are merely just words, not even worth spelling out, separated from my experience. Empty.

Now, that I have decided to settle in this city, at least for the foreseeable future. Now, that it has started – that which I can't name. Now, that I've reached this junction.

My sip – as though to draw a line – turns out much more hectic than planned:

"So, tell me more about your work."

"Do I have to?"

"Is it that bad?"

"No."

"So?"

I lean onto my elbows. My unremarkable outfit – black sleeveless top, blue jeans, almost no make-up – was chosen for yet another stranger, yet another night, not *this*. My hair is bound together in a careless bundle of brown, revealing ears without earrings. I wasn't in the mood for tonight at all.

He looks almost over-dressed in comparison. His pale grey shirt is a perfect fit, its sleeves folded up once or twice. I caught a glimpse of his neat black jeans when he rose from the table to greet me. I was almost fifteen minutes late.

"It's just that... Why don't you tell me more about your work instead?"

"Because working in politics is so much more interesting than the meaningless editorial assistant job I have accepted, don't you think?"

"No."

"No?"

"In any case, I'm as much an assistant as you are. Which is to say: I get to see all the dirt, without being able to make any decisions myself."

I uncross my arms and place my hands the way his hands are placed, to the left and to the right of his plate, far too calm, unfairly at ease.

"Would you like to do that?"

"Make decisions? Isn't that what politics is all about? I thought anyway. Unfortunately, there's so much at work that prevents us from... Anyway, boring. Let's not talk about it. My job's on my mind too much as it is."

"What's on your mind?"

"Right now?"

There's a second of surprise, a mild shock that's flashing through him, but he suppresses the reflex quicker than I can regret my sudden advance.

I had no say in this; my reaching-out just happened.

"You're warm."

"Sweaty, you mean. I'm sorry about that."

He shakes his head. His thumb feels soft against my skin. He's moving it now, very gently.

Of course I neither mentioned the unhelpful behaviour of my hands, nor that of my cheeks on the site that brought us to this tiny table-for-two. There was no field dedicated to reactions when placed under emotional stress, no box to be ticked for my affinity to show when something actually matters.

I move my glance along his arms and across his shirt – towards the danger zone.

I've stopped seeing the particulars of it almost immediately – his distinct chin, the way his nose meets his lightly coloured lips, his clean-shaven, cared for skin – and started taking in this harmony, like sips from my wine, his dark blond hair in a beautiful duet with his eyes, which are unusually green and mysterious in a way things are that invite you without allowing you in fully.

Would I have taken my place on this table-for-two had I known this would happen? No.

But my bum is on my chair; there's nothing I can do: *Sign Out* is no longer on my menu bar.

I move my second hand forwards and touch him a bit more firmly.

He smiles:

"Are you doing this often, then? I wanted to ask you."

"Touching people's hands?"

"Dating."

"God, I hate the word. But no... I mean, yes, for a few months now. Before I came to this city things just happened. But now? I don't know. It's all a little... sad."

"Sad?"

"I'm probably using that word too often. It's just that... I don't know."

It's just that I've seen too much recently, sitting down in restaurants that looked as non-specific and bland as this one, untangling what had been obscured beforehand over another glass of house wine, picking up the pieces over pizza, wondering how I'm supposed to connect to anyone like this, veiled by exaggerated expectation.

Soon, I guess, our phones will drill into us on the back of some secret algorithm, answering all the questions before they have been asked, but in the second decade of the twenty-first century this still has to be done the hard way.

But tonight is nothing like that. That's the problem. Our fingers are playing with each other.

It's not just that he didn't ask about what you're supposed to ask about on occasions like this: my favourite bands and my favourite films and my favourite this and that – I can never decide and that's hardly helped if I'm being asked to do it from the top of my head and what's that supposed to say about me anyway?

It's not just that he consciously avoided the topics that could have come to him all too easily, the state of our world according to him; a dreaded intellectual show-off was being replaced by a refreshing curiosity for what makes me tick, and, being asked like that, I even found the words, for a change.

It's not just that everything that happened between us just happened; all I had to do was to lean forward and let it happen. And every minute that passed on our tiny table-for-two increased the shock to my unprepared system.

My nose is almost close enough to come up against his now. If I wanted to, my lips could find out whether he tastes the way he looks. My eyes – drifting over his right shoulder – pull me even closer towards them.

Behind the window that's in his back are the streets, neon lights and shop fronts that make up this city – and yet what I see is more. And yet, what I see is less. And I'm still only getting my head around that myself.

His hand is on my naked arm now, slowly crawling forward. I'm enjoying every finger.

My mind is being traversed by alleyways that become highways, by cycle lanes that are rivers, by canals that morph into tree-lined promenades. The parks in this city are the parks of my past, all in one, the squares my squares, merged. All my rivers are flowing into each other.

His hand has reached my elbow; mine is where the sleeve of his shirt blocks my way.

Everything that felt so distinct about a city at the time – the texture of its pavements, the font on its street signs, the shine of its night – now it's all lost, like flotsam.

To me, the city I have decided to settle in, at least for the foreseeable future, seems to be what my rational self knows it isn't: towering but flat, straight and confused, sprawling yet enclosed. And there's nothing I can do. *This* city is my reality now, what surrounds me: all I've got.

His eyes meet mine as though he's been exactly where I have been, and I refuse to believe that it's possible to fake attention and appreciation on that level. There wasn't a moment of boredom on his face in the last two hours and I had almost forgotten how much harm that can do.

"Hot in here, isn't it?"

"Not really, no. But if you're referring to your cheeks, don't worry. I like them like that."

"Hey, I wasn't –"

"But not just like that."

I stare at him.

"And not just them."

This is too much. I want to say things I cannot say. I want to do things I cannot do. I no longer understand.

"Thanks for making it worse."

"I'm sorry."

"No, you're not."

"No, I'm not."

I shake my head. It has to come out of his mouth any minute now – the one sentence that will tell me that this isn't worth the effort, that this is a terrible waste of time, just like before. He has to say it, sooner or later – the one word that will debunk this encounter for what it really is, a big fat cliché. Too good to be true. I tighten my grip.

"What's wrong?"

"Nothing."

"You're sure?"

I nod, slowly. It spares me another lie.

His eyes are resting on my lips now, as though in encouragement – but I stay silent.

Secretly, of course, I want this evening to last until we have exhausted each other totally, until we have greedily sucked up every last bit of telling detail, of useful information, of simple beauty, but I'm beginning to understand that only a swift departure from this table-for-two will make another table-for-two inevitable and that only another table-for-two will give me a chance to find out what I won't be able to find out tonight.

I let my hand glide back over his arms, moving him away from my elbow.

Only our fingers are still touching now. I lean back.

I need to get us out of our romantic corner, slash the flirty haze we're in. But how?

Somehow, my intellect needs to come back, and cool this overheated machine with a heavy dose of fact, a splash of cold water against my face, red cheeks steaming. I need to be ruthless. I don't think twice:

"So, what do you think about climate change?"

2

We are no longer using the phrase; no one here is. Like its partner in crime, global warming, it's never been any good at describing what's actually going on – right now, not in a hundred years. Both terms have always been a little too vague to hit what actually needs to be hit, and, criminally abused and overused, became mere phrases, a switch-off. So we decided, collectively as it were, to name the issues instead.

We have moved on; we are that way.

We? That's something I would never have thought I would become a part of. Not in my wildest dreams.

Two months ago, all this was far away – time-wise, geographically, from my life. I wasn't ignorant, but I didn't see how any of it touched me, even just marginally. Two months ago, all this was other people, elsewhere, and I didn't give a shit, really.

We – that's a small miracle.

It's taking place – almost every night now – in a small room that would be easier to describe if there was anything to describe: a large wooden table and a few chairs, found and fixed – that's it. The only natural light comes through a small window that's located just below the ceiling, the only heating is provided by our own breathing bodies. The room's walls are so cold and bare they freaked me out for a long time at the beginning, but now – as with so many other things – that feels just normal.

We – that's four others and me.

It might seem odd to call them the way I do – there's the ex-banker, there's the fashionista, there's the brain and there's our leader – but it helps me, and I think it helps them too. Most importantly, though, it helps us, I think: It strengthens our We – the We that has moved beyond parts per million, the We that has moved beyond degrees.

Inside the bare room, we have stored away the charts, because the charts, by now, are an integral part of us, each and every one of us. We know about feedback loops and knock-on effects, but we know even more how pointless it is to get lost in discussions about them. We have seen the scenarios and the modelling, but we know that scenarios and modelling are just that, scenarios and modelling. But if we have moved on, then so has the world…

What's happening right now is there for everyone to see: the system is heating up. A fine balance is being unsettled, and not without consequences.

Why? There's no doubt about that anymore either. Far too much has happened for that in the last two months.

At this point, only one question needs to be resolved, and that's exactly what our We is all about: How can we stop making it worse as quickly as possible?

I can't believe I'm talking like this, but I am.

3

"Alone? That early?"

I was hoping my two flatmates would be fast asleep by now. Unfortunately, it's not the quiet one either, still sitting in our kitchen, but her outspoken counterpart:

"Another failure of a male human being, then?"

She's looking at me, but I'm still standing outside the restaurant, holding his gaze. My abrupt change of topic did what I wanted it to do, even though I'm not sure what exactly it did to him; something serious?

We left twenty minutes later, not even bothering with coffee.

"Hello, hello?"

I can still feel it, first left, then right, and then – there wasn't a hint of the clumsy, unattractive uncertainty that often destroys all sense of attraction in a moment like this.

My flatmate is waving at me, but I'm looking right through her. He could have kissed me, of course. Easily. I wouldn't have resisted. He must have felt that.

But he didn't. And what he did was so much better. I can still see the decisiveness in his eyes, the way he said, without opening his mouth, that he had no intention to abuse the occasion, lazily sealing the night with what could have been the end-of-story. That he wanted this occasion to be a beginning instead. I can still see the smile that stayed on his face as he turned, finally.

"Hey, are you still here?"

I shake my head.

A grown-up, un-arrogant confidence mixed with a hint of desire. A mere hint – a teaser that was so much stronger than the real thing could have been.

"Well, I can see that. Not such a failure of a male human being, then, I take it?"

"Sorry, I don't feel like talking right now. I'll tell you all about it tomorrow, okay?"

"Boring, boring, boring. Okay."

I walk over to the sink, fill a glass with water and walk out of the kitchen without another word.

I know, of course, that turning away before anything has started would be the only sensible behaviour at this point. So much effort is needed for two people to reach the point where what's going on can justifiably be called meaningful – and so much disappointment will cloud your days when it all goes wrong just before you reach that point – it's worth considering the daring leap that's required to start getting there about a hundred and two times before you actually make it. I know that letting go is the biggest risk you can take in life, and I know that you take it at your own peril. I have experience; I have my rules. I come fully prepared. I know that I am as far from doing this lightly as you can possibly be.

If only there wasn't, in these eyes, a promise I haven't seen in anyone's eyes for years.

I close my room door, leaning against it from behind. My room – that's a bed and a bunch of boxes I still haven't unpacked. Four months. What's four months?

No desk, no shelf, not even a wardrobe. My dresses, tops and jumpers all hang from an open metal rail. Everything else is still stored in suitcases and bags underneath – a situation I curse every morning. There's no decoration on any of the room's dark blue walls. There's not even a bedside table.

I could easily make this my home, of course. I would merely have to accept it is, first.

I walk over to the bed, which is located in the far corner, just beneath the window that's giving way to our flat-share's small garden. I sit down, facing the dark room.

A familiar melody is coming up against my back. The sounds are unmistakably the sounds of this city – the dying hum of the midnight traffic, interspersed with a siren, here and there, and a steady late wind – but I can hear all my others in there too.

It's the same with smells. Sometimes a whiff on a corner is enough to take me by the hand, and back five years. The smell of a city is made up of a thousand different notes and touches and hints and yet: it's unique. And once you have been breathing it, it stays with you forever.

I close my eyes, but they pop up again, immediately: A simple brown? Believe me, he said, they are so much more than a simple brown.

I can't help it. I'm looking at his smile again and it's enough for my imagination to take me by the my hand, and I'm perfectly conscious it's happening, but I'm not resisting, for a change – and it freaks me out.

I'm being whirled up into a sphere, where sense is out of stock and borders don't exist, and I'm not getting in the way – because, up here, on the other side of my resistance, somehow, someone is insisting that this isn't going to be another modified version of what's littering my past already.

I close my eyes, but they pop up again, immediately.

4

Journeys. That's how I like to think about the relationships I had in the last ten years.

Some of them were so shallow I can't recall them now and seriously wonder why I bothered then. Others were just about committed enough to deserve their name. All of them lasted just as long as I wanted them to last, simmering on, conveniently, until I decided – always in charge; the way I liked it – that it was time for another departure, that I had to move on, a line-up of well-rehearsed excuses at hand, no time for scenes, tears or a discussion.

To me, split-ups were like business transactions. My entire love life was based on contracts that had get-out clauses so obviously favouring me over whoever found himself at the other end it's hard to believe anyone agreed to them, but they all did. The kind ones and the good-looking ones. The supportive ones and the desperate ones. Cap in hand, they all joined into how I was doing things, pragmatically slithering in and out of these would-be connections in the name of a holy principle, flexibility.

And there was nothing wrong with that, nothing at all. Until I moved to this city. Until I reached this junction.

Ever since, something I never really cared for has grown into a desire that's running so deep it's hard to control, and, whether I like it or not, it keeps spreading, almost painfully, and a little more with every day that passes. Why else would I be giving myself up to the ordeal of dating?

It's the desire for a burning heart.

5

"What are the power station people saying?"

"The usual."

"Any other reactions?"

"Politicians saying that they are taking this very seriously?"

"God. I don't know why we even still mention the kind of shit they're coming up with."

"Because we need them."

"Is the problem exactly, isn't it?"

"Three thousand of us are putting ourselves in the way of a monstrous wrong, and all they come up with is the usual phrase about taking this seriously?"

"Yes, I mean, they're politicians. Aren't they supposed to take things seriously?"

"Aren't they supposed to do so much more?"

The five of us are standing around the table. Our words are bouncing between us, filling the bare room with a humming, like low-level electricity. The air smells of exhaustion.

"They've become pretty good at paying lip service, that's all, given all that has happened in the last two months."

"Yes, and behind their backs? Seriously my arse."

"Absolutely. I mean, they're happily handing out permits for exactly this kind of plant elsewhere."

"And allow whatever digging, drilling or fracking suits our needs, yes. It's a joke. It's sickening."

"Not to mention the billions in worldwide subsidies and tax breaks that still have the fossil fuel industry's bosses scream Hallelujah all the way to their next shareholder meeting."

"Three thousand people – hand in hand. The pictures are so beautiful, aren't they? We're all over the feed."

Someone's phone, lying on the table, is displaying *#coalchain*.

"Any arrests, actually?"

"Not that I know of."

"Some of the high-profile guys out there in prison, that would be something, wouldn't it?"

A deep breath fills the room. We're all hearing it. And then we're all hearing:

"People. If you start talking about others going to prison, you should start with yourself. I've said this before, but I will say it again:

Unless you're prepared to go there yourself you have no right to talk that way."

He looks at us from behind his horn-rimmed glasses. It's the clichéd facade for his brain – the massive, scary brain that understands everything to its last consequence, parts per million, knock-on effects and feedback loops; the brain that made Fourier, Tyndall and Arrhenius accessible to me and got me to understand what's rising where and why and what the hell it all means.

He's crouching on his chair the usual way, unaware of his bad posture, the sort of slump that comes with introspection taken to its limit: a thinker's disease. I sometimes wonder if he sits like this at work too, the think tank on a Green New Deal that prides itself with his name, or if this is behaviour restricted to the bare room, just like most of what he's saying in here is, the think tank blissfully unaware of these extra-curricular activities.

He looks at us the way he likes to look at us in moments like this, the black skin of his forehead in wrinkles of scepticism, the challenge of a critic who knows exactly what he's talking about whenever he's talking about anything.

Next to him, the ex-banker is leaning back casually, his legs apart, man-style, grinning. He looks even more gelled than usual today, his blond hair spiked skywards, and once again, I can't help notice the oddness of him being here, of all places, but then again, the same could be said about me.

In a way, it makes perfect sense: He was released from his duties when the great experiment went bad last time round, he told me. Since then, he said, he had too much time to learn what he had been doing all those years, playing with what, to him, had only been numbers, and learn what, inevitably, had stood behind them: lives. He had too much time to realise, he said, that all those years he had been duped by a system that was designed to serve no one but those operating it and that he wanted no part in it anymore.

So here he is.

Even though, I'm not sure what exactly he's looking for, here. What really drives him.

An awkward silence fills the room. Next to the ex-banker, there's the fashionista in our ranks, all bright greens and yellows today in a combination no on else in this room would dare. She's preparing one of her self-rolled cigarettes, licking the thin paper.

Her lips are in a red that is, as usual, in a perfect harmony with her creamy dark skin.

She's smirking at the brain as though to say that we had this discussion many times before and that there's no point having it again now, but the brain isn't looking at her or the ex-banker or me, but at the one person in here we all see as our leader, even though, on paper, there isn't supposed to be one.

Her fiery red curls are half obscuring a face that's clearly agitated about not having an answer to a question we have all pondered, I'm sure, without reaching a satisfactory answer – at least not as far as I'm concerned: We are asking a lot. How far are we, ourselves, prepared to go?

"How was the demonstration on the weekend? Sorry I couldn't make it, in the end."

"Great mix, once again. Church guys marching arm in arm with union folks. They really seem to be picking this up. A few hundred thousand, once again."

"Reactions?"

"None?"

"Shit. And I thought I'd come here today for some good news."

"Not the feel-good department, this, I'm afraid."

"I know that much by now."

But I can't help feeling that we've been moving in a circle. It's not that the last few meetings weren't productive – we got down brilliantly how fossil fuels made us who we are; how it's been a hell of a ride; how we wouldn't have wanted to miss it; how it's got to be over – but I feel that we've become a bit obsessed with coal, in particular.

I can't help feeling that we're stuck, but I don't say anything – I'm still the newcomer to the group, after all. And besides, I haven't found a different way forward myself, have I?

Sometimes, when I'm sleepless in my bed, or dreamy on a bus to work, I imagine the five of us at the centre of something really momentous, something that will take everyone's breath away. I never quite know how to picture it, but every time it happens, the thought seems a little less far-fetched. It might happen, I tell myself, and sometimes: It will.

"I really don't get it!"

Our leader bangs her fist on table the way she sometimes does.

"What are these politicians? Blind? Deaf? Dumb? All the above? How long will they get away with pretending that nothing has happened?"

6

This is what happened: Two months ago, a group of international scientists decided to take their insides out – and not just out of their shielded back rooms, their tucked-away studies, but right onto the big stage. Where everyone could see.

You don't have to *believe* in anything, they said. You just have to take a good look.

Those who know better than anyone what's happening to our world took the charts that wake them at night and showed them to the masses. Those who used to be a weird abstraction had flesh and blood, families and children, stories and jokes.

Some of those first appearances were awkward, of course. Long-winded answers to simple questions turned audiences away, discouraged the untrained speakers, got some to reconsider. But this transition didn't last long. With every appearance, their strength grew. With every show, their skills got refined, their stamina increased. Every mention on the feed fired them, and it wasn't long until those that had taken the first courageous step into the spotlight started experiencing the inevitable: They wanted more. What had been written off as of no interest – now it was a super show.

The best we, as humans, can do regained the status it had long lost to other fancies, flimsy concepts, trash, and it did so right at the centre of our attention. The facts that make up the very foundation of our future – suddenly, they were no longer just theirs.

Suddenly, they were no longer someone's, anyone's. Suddenly, they were ours.

Shortly afterwards, those who did so much to destroy what used to be a consensus – viciously twisting a few selected facts to distort, in our eyes, decades of scientific achievement – finally got what they deserved.

It was their selfish propaganda, and the faux debate it caused, that had kept me away from the issue altogether, a bunch of greying men in suits arguing over numbers. Who cares!

Three leaks – that was all it took in the end. So exorbitant were the sums of money that had flown, for years, from industries and individuals with stakes in the status quo so high it wasn't surprising they were prepared to pay them; so shocking were the levels of sheer corruption; so obvious was the self-interest behind every sentence of denial ever uttered, public opinion finally, and forever, swung against those who fabricated discord where it had no place. Abusing the term sceptical for no one's benefit, but their own.

These words are my words, unlikely as they may feel. That's our We too. That's me:

In a play involving all of us, these villains had been allowed to wear the borrowed robes of scepticism for too long, but suddenly it was over. Suddenly, these self-appointed preacher men of money had no one to shout their untruths at, but one another, and that's where they still are now, in their dirty little corner, slowly sinking into their quicksand of deception, counting their money in loneliness.

That's what happened in the last two months: The If made way for the How, once and for all. Sadly, it didn't make the How any easier, though, did it?

7

Our leader is standing now. She's wearing her trademark hooded jumper in black, washed-out jeans, mock-Converse. Her red curls are unruly on either side.

Our positions are unchanged. So is the air in here. The ex-banker is looking at me:

"You're very quiet today."

"Am I?"

"Yes. What's up?"

He lifts his right leg and moves it into its default position, its ankle resting on the other knee, teetering, nervously:

"Fallen in love, finally?"

All I can do is to stare at him in disbelief; I should never have told him I was dating.

"She's fallen in love!"

"Shut up... What is this, kindergarten?"

He keeps grinning. It's his nonchalant sense of superiority, his special brand of mild male arrogance, that has prevented me from embracing the ex-banker as much as I have embraced the fashionista or the brain. It's not a disliking, really – I do like him, in the harmless way you like someone who's good fun to be with. It's just that, with him, there's a little more distance. A bit more caution.

"Tell us more."

"I met someone, yes, but I don't see what's the big deal. And I have no idea how you've seen it."

"Male intuition, ever heard about that?"

"Male intuition?"

"Yes, it's not a female-only domain, that. Common misconception."

"You can spare us your gender philosophy, okay? Who is he?"

The fashionista.

They're all staring at me now, waiting – even the brain, who is not usually romantically inclined.

Today is Monday. Our date was on Saturday. I would like to pretend it's not true, but there weren't many hours in between I didn't think of him at least once. Even now, during our conversation his face didn't quite leave my head. The ex-banker wasn't all that wrong. There might be some sense for the female condition mixed with his macho-tendencies, after all.

"I'll tell you another time, okay? It's all very fresh and –"

"Fair enough."

Our leader is keen to steer the conversation back to where it matters for her. The others need and welcome a little distraction every now and again as much as I do, I think, especially when things get too heated, or too hopeless – but she doesn't. And today I'm with her.

I received a text message just as I entered the room, but I promised myself not to look at it until after our session. I keep fiddling the phone in my pocket in nervous anticipation.

I lean forward:

"I think there's simply not enough people on board. Still. Something isn't quite sparking."

The fashionista crosses her leggings:

"Hundred thousands on the street again – hello?"

"All nice and fine, yes, but what's a few hundred thousands? If you think about the scale of the problem."

"As I've been saying: As long as my grandmother doesn't get this, we don't stand a chance."

The ex-banker laughs out loud, saying it. He has his arms crossed in front of his stripy white shirt now.

"And not just get it. We need your grandmother to climb that power plant, don't we?"

"That'd be a good one. Have you seen her recently?"

The brain breaks between them:

"No we don't. All we need is enough people feeling strongly enough to punish politicians come election time."

Our leader:

"Yes, but when's election time? Can we really wait until all the countries around us have election time at some point in the future? Plus, party programmes are complex. I mean, who's really speaking up for this? And as far as punishment is concerned, I just haven't seen an awful lot of it recently, have you?"

"She's right. This world's politicians are resigning over private property affairs, academic plagiarism, extramarital affairs, wrongly filled-in expense claims and illegal phone tapping, but they clearly aren't resigning over this. Yet."

Me.

Sometimes, I find it hard to believe it's only been two months for me in here. The four of them seem sweetly familiar, by now – the brain and his habit of underlining everything with a report, a study so long and dry only he would read it. The ex-banker and his brashness, the loud and unrestrained way he has to whip us into excitement. The fashionista and her casual way of bringing our lofty debates down to earth, where people actually live. And the leader and her conviction, the current that is running through everything she says and does, the drive that infuses the entire group, again and again, with a sense of how much this actually matters.

And yet, I know almost nothing about them. Still.

We – that also means leaving your nationality, your past and your prejudices at the door of the room.

It was the only rule I was given, when I joined, and we are all adhering to it, rigorously. It has suited me just fine, of course: At no point was I cross-examined about the last ten years, did I have to lie about my junction, was there a need to admit that I'm my own worst consequence, a product of my decisions, belonging nowhere at all.

There are moments when I feel I'd like to know more about the others, but then I also feel that, somehow, less knowledge makes them more human, in a way, and the more I think about it, the more sense it makes.

"What we need is people influencing those in power without an election. This isn't about changing the government, but about changing the government, if you know what I mean. That's the mission here, people."

The brain's black skin is in wrinkles again; he knows how hard a mission this really is.

He rolls up the sleeve that has fallen down too far from the way he likes to wear it. His shirt is a nice grey and, annoyingly, reminds me of the shirt he was wearing.

The ex-banker shoots his finger at him:

"Led by my grandmother!"

"Sure."

"Problem is: My grandmother isn't on board."

"Because you haven't properly explained to her what this is all about."

"Have you done that with yours? I bet you haven't even talked to your parents about this properly."

"Well."

I wonder if that isn't true for all of us? I know it's true for me, at least. They wouldn't understand, I keep telling myself, even though I know that's merely a convenient way to ignore the real reason – the reason I'm trying not to think about. One day, I keep telling myself. One day.

The ex-banker shakes his head:

"Explaining, explaining, explaining won't get us anywhere in the end. As far as I'm concerned, we need to be much bolder. I will keep saying this. We need to go much further."

"But what does that mean?"

"I don't know – encircle coal power stations not just for a day or a night, but for weeks. Something a bit more –"

"Unfortunately, too many people still perceive this as unnecessary trouble making."

"Jesus."

"Yes, but remember, it's not just about how we see the world. It's about how everyone else sees the world too."

It's something the brain keeps saying.

"I know, I know, but if we're not prepared to go up a step, then, I don't know. A few months ago, encircling a power station was still a big deal. I mean, we were all there. But now it's happening all the time. Does it make a difference? It makes fuck all of a difference, is what it makes. Look out. I mean, really."

The ex-banker pauses, then:

"I mean, I could suggest something."

He looks at us, from me to the brain and then to the leader, but neither of us responds.

He has tried this a few times, recently, and I was never quite sure what to make of it.

He casually touches the fashionista's leg with his, but that only triggers a sigh, and there's no overhearing the hint of irritation in it. She gets up, as though to make a point:

"Seriously, what are we to do?"

"Yeah, what's next?"

"I don't know."

"No idea."

"Haven't got a clue."

"Hurray. And once again, this room has reached a point where the impossibility of this endeavour is so obvious I just want to get up and leave. Ladies and gentleman, we've run out of ideas. Bring out the bottle. Let's drink."

"Shut it."

"No, but there's hope."

"Thanks."

"Why don't we paint that on the walls here?"

"Because it's a waste of paint?"

"No, it's not. It's good to be reminded. You know how easy it is to turn away. To shut off. I think we need to give ourselves some more credit for not doing so."

"Self-applauding doesn't get us anywhere."

"No, it doesn't. But it prevents us from going the other way, at least."

It's a brave brain, conquering our leader's harsh stance on this. She keeps repeating it, but they are both right, I think.

My glance wanders from the fashionista – who has stuck her perfectly rolled cigarette between her lips as though to make the point that she'd rather be out smoking than further engage in this pointless talk – to the ex-banker, who was looking at her, but knows better than to waste my eye contact:

"Meeting him again, then?"

"Who?"

"Your new man."

"I don't know. Maybe... I haven't..."

The bare room was my attempt to ban, if only for an hour or two, the fragments that are still hopping around inside of me. Our table-for-two keeps replaying in flashes of excitement that have the power to tickle me into exhaustion and it's happening far too frequently, given who I am. Given all I know.

What might he be up to right now? What might he be up to later in the week?

I'm dying to read that text message.

"What does he do?"

"What?"

"What does he work, I mean."

"Why don't we just get back to the business of this room?"

"Come on. What is he, an estate agent?"

"No, he isn't. He works in politics."

"He works in politics!"

"What kind?"

"He's only an assistant... but, he's... it's close to the environmental department."

"The. Environmental. Department."

Our leader is suddenly very interested in a distraction that isn't a distraction any longer. She crosses her arms in front of her curvy chest. I shake my head, weirdly:

"It doesn't mean much. It's just a job for him. He's far away from the action."

"That's what they all say."

"And he's very disillusioned with his job."

"I bet he is. So what does he do, apart from looking at how the planet's going to hell in a handcart?"

"That's not fair."

"Not fair? You know, that's the problem, exactly. We keep talking about the politicians, this, the politicians, that. We curse them and hate them and whatever, but as soon as they stop being this convenient abstraction we create for ourselves, then we're suddenly too shy to touch them. What's the problem? If he's working in the environmental department and isn't doing anything then he's as guilty as the big ones are, isn't he?"

"Well, maybe, yes... Anyway, I'm not going to talk to you about someone I have only just met. Once."

"Exactly, how unfair is that."

"I wasn't meant to be unfair. I was just saying. Why don't you bring him in?"

"What, here?"

The brain, adjusting his horn-rimmed glasses, and the ex-banker, nervously scratching the spiky blond hair behind his right ear, and the fashionista, taking out her perfectly rolled cigarette again, all mirror her look in anticipation:

"Could be interesting, no?"

8

Nothing would have happened without her. Nothing. The scientists stepping up – nice and fine. The deniers falling down – helpful. The artists who are pushing the issue into new, unexplored territory, relentlessly competing for the freshest approach, the most fruitful take – interesting. All the organisations and activists, camps and communities that have been active on this for years – really, really admirable. But all that wouldn't have touched me. Not in the slightest.

It took a party of a friend of a friend, two months ago, where I stood, on my own, captivated by the view that came with the host's fourteenth-floor flat.

It's really weird, she said, out of nowhere, suddenly standing next to me, gazing out:

One part of me wants to switch off all these lights right now. Just think of all the energy that's flowing through these buildings. Just think of all the waste. Can you imagine it? All the waste, right there, in front of our eyes.

I turned, surprised by the approach, and that's when I saw her red curls for the first time. It's such a distinct look, her blue eyes perpetually interchanging between friendly and furious, her pale white skin not quite giving away the passion that's perfectly visible, nevertheless, in her commanding voice and in her posture. Domineering without being overpowering.

The other part tells me to shut the fuck up, she said, because it's just so beautiful. And that's only one of many contradictions.

It was the first time I met someone who cared passionately for the environment – that mystical construct, which, for me, had always been a vague out-there, somewhere far away – and at the same time displayed, without even a hint of shame, a lust for a life based on so many of the things I thought to be problematic when you do. She's a walking mass of contradictions, and she didn't even think of making an excuse for it.

How could you be an environmentalist and concede that you could never live close to nature? That the city – with its pollution, its light waste, its feverish deconstruction and reconstruction, its never-ending production of rubbish – is the only place you can function.

Don't call me an environmentalist, she said, that's such a stupidly restricting label.

How could you hate cars and admire the beauty in a freeway? How could you be aware of aviation's destructive impact, yet salute the international airport as your favourite location on the planet? How could you be at the very forefront of this fight without ridding yourself of all that first?

That's exactly the problem, she said. If we expect people to shed all their links to the life we've grown used to, to everything we do, before they join the fight, no one will ever sign up. We will never get anywhere. We need to start from where we are, not where we want to be. We need to be honest. We need to admit that all this is as fucking difficult for me as it is for you, as it is for everyone.

Talking to her that night was like being led, ever so casually, around a house you have only ever seen from its front, so you can take a look at its back, and then, if you want to, approach a window you didn't even know existed – for a peek, no more. And I only allowed being led like that because she seemed the most unlikely person to say any of the things she was saying to me, jumping from sentence to sentence without a breath.

Gazing at the lights of our city – she with her cheap can of beer, me with my glass of red wine – she told me how she had realised that it was time to stop treating this as some minor side issue people chose to care about, or not, depending on what their favourite celebrity said about it, and that she had recently down-graded her job as a supermarket cashier from full-time to part-time to devote even more time to making sure we did.

I'm not really an activist, she said, though I know quite a few people who are, in the tents and beyond, and I really adore them. But personally I'm just an ordinary working women, you know what I mean?

It was her strength and her confidence, but even more, I think, her down-to-earth nature that kept me listening, and talking.

By the time we exchanged mobile numbers, a subject that had been a mere dot at the periphery of my conscience had started, ever so slowly, to move towards it's centre; the process had begun. Behind the window, a plane crossed the night time sky, its red/white lights flashing.

And yet, there was also something about this women I didn't quite get. Something I couldn't quite trust?

9

Perhaps it has been an illusion, after all. I'm sitting on my bed, cross-legged, with my mobile in my hand and my hand in my lap. Outside, it's getting dark. Perhaps, he didn't even feel a fraction of what I felt during those two hours?

The text message I fiddled for hours in the bare room turned out to be not from him, but from my quiet flatmate: We're out of toilet paper, can you bring some?

It's Wednesday by now. Perhaps our table-for-two meant nothing to him? Perhaps I deluded myself terribly.

I switch tabs on my phone to have another look at the feed, displaying *#coalchain*. It's been going on for three days now, and the feed is still awash with frontline takes:

Standing here with pensioners, school children and one of my favourite football players. Feeling great.

The brain called me about it this morning and talked, unusually enthusiastically, about the diversity of those involved, the shift system that has been conceived on the spot, the rational arguments that are being made by people from all walks of life, before he returned to his default dryness and said that, realistically, we will not see a wider reaction to this, despite what he said was decent mainstream media coverage.

There's no mistaking this: The mainstream media, too, have changed in the last few months. I know this because the brain knows this. My media consumption is like most people's, these days, restricted to the micro-stream that has replaced the mainstream, our individualised provision, but his job requires our premium thinker to read, or at least scan, the mainstream press every morning and he told me all about it the other day.

We were sitting in the bare room, just the two of us, waiting for the rest, killing silence:

What do you mean, the wave?

It's what they call it. It's the direction everyone's writing in, if you like.

Can you write in a direction?

It's what's expected. Or what the journalists and editors of the world think is expected. What I mean to say is that, in the last few months, a few of them have started to somehow write... against it. If only very carefully. And only a few. But there's potential.

His dark black hair is cut extremely short. This is where he scratched it, letting the word potential hang in the room. He looks smart even in a light-blue shirt that could have done with some ironing, I thought. His dark blue jeans – they're all second-hand, he keeps insisting – gave way to a pair of barefoot-style shoes in olive green.

No question, the coldness that dominated our relationship in the very beginning – he distrusted my city-hopping lifestyle, I think, as much as I distrusted his elite education and the resulting accent, however softly spoken it is – has made way for something much warmer in recent weeks. And yet, sometimes, I'm still not quite sure about the brain. It's still hard for me to see the man behind the facts and his figures, the soul amid the sanity.

But he's right. The issue is only waiting to be claimed. Isn't this set to become *the* area, touching everyone equally? All we need is for the bandwagon to start rolling, I guess. For a few troublemakers to break the worst habits, for a bunch of angry young journalists to ditch a few archaic rules. Maybe, he said.

The brain is easily the most sceptical of us, but I guess that's just because he knows so much.

The fashionista sent me one of her stream-of-consciousness texts from her boutique shift earlier, but she, too, left no doubt about her fear that nothing would come of the chain.

And still, as much as those with an interest to do so are trying to ignore what's been going on, and paint the best direct action so far as a street carnival, nice but without meaning, I can't help feeling that the bar has been raised, ever so slightly.

I'm convinced: The consequences of this *will* be felt, whatever is being said now.

I place my phone in my lap and stare into the room. There isn't even a TV in here, which, I was surprised to hear, is true for every member of our group expect the ex-banker, who likes to watch the football – a close second, he says, to the collection of obscure science fiction comics on his list of hobbies, which, he says, features two hobbies in total.

The lonely CFL that dangles from my ceiling without a shade radiates a clinical brightness that only adds to the feeling of for-now that permeates my room.

I hit the switch that's above my bed and ask the darkness, as it falls: Why is it that we're so bad at handling you? Why is it that we're so bad at handling silence?

I turn away. In a moment like this, it seems as though the tree we have in our garden isn't just overlooking me, but looking *at* me, it's branches an open invitation to drift...

It takes me four or five rings to realise what's happening, both darkness and silence: gone. Hastily, I move the phone where it needs to be:

"Hi... I mean, hello... Hi!"

I can't believe he's calling me! Calling me, not sending a text – what character!

"I hope I'm not disturbing you? I thought you wouldn't pick up..."

"Not at all. Disturbing me, I mean."

Stop grinning, girl. I need to stop grinning. I can hear it in my own voice.

"It's just that... I don't know how you felt last time, but I had a great time and... I was wondering if you might want to meet for dinner again, perhaps?"

Stay calm.

"Absolutely. I mean, yes... That would be very nice. When's good for you?"

"How about Saturday again?"

How about tomorrow!

"Sure."

"It's just that it's very busy at work at the moment, so the weekend's better for me. It's all a bit mad here right now, if you know what I mean."

"Yes, that's fine. Saturday's great. Where shall we go?"

"I have a place in mind. I'll text you the address later, okay? Surprise."

"I like that."

"I'm looking forward to it."

"Yes."

Yes? Is that all you have to say? Yes?

"Okay, well, see you Saturday."

"See you Saturday, yes... and..."

"Yes?"

"Thanks for calling."

"Sure."

My display morphs back to the feed, where *#coalchain* keeps delivering its arguments for moving away from fossil fuels as quickly as possible, but I'm still seeing his soft, lightly coloured lips, smiling at me the way they did last week.

I'm grinning at my phone in the starry-eyed stupor of a pubescent teenager. I had a great time, he said. Saturday, he said. I'm looking forward to it, he said. My phone starts to fade, but my expression doesn't follow suit.

My eyelids, as they close, tenderly conceal a mind that's already skipping a few days.

10

I wonder whether, on our last table-for-two, he noticed my language. How I'm slowly losing it.

Ever since I made a different one the main subject of my studies, the way I speak got diluted, a little more, I think, with every country I lived in. At first, I started to miss words. Then, sentences began to break, refused to end. In order not to embarrass myself totally, I started using whatever came easiest, borrowed, adapted and tweaked and that's when everything crossed over, blended and reacted. That's when, slowly, everything collapsed.

What used to be one of my best traits, full of charm and wit and natural warmth, has become a backbone, no more. My language has become the ugly scaffolding that holds together my speech, just about. The awkward muddle that's only still itself in my thoughts, and on the page. Where no one is listening; where my weird creations and strange pictures don't bother anyone; where I can edit myself into something that's deemed half-way acceptable.

In my thoughts, and on the page, things are different – special, even, at times – but as soon as the words start leaving my mouth, they become the embarrassing stuttering of a modern-day vagabond, the most obvious hint at my disintegrating inner state.

Didn't I tell him far too much about it on our last table-for-two? I really wonder.

Wasn't it a real risk for me to go on, the way I did, about my once-customary getting there, always one step ahead of myself, and about my constant state of becoming, becoming, becoming? How now, here, at this, my junction, there isn't any of it left. Didn't he understand me far too well?

Now, here, I'm being asked to just *be* – and sometimes it's just too much to take. But I didn't tell him that. I stopped myself just in time. Because that's where the real trouble starts.

11

"Where're you off to?"

My quiet flatmate raises her head as I pass through the kitchen, leaving a trail of too much rose with a hint of amber.

"Actually, I think I know."

This is a terrible idea. I should never have taken his number, should never have given him mine.

Meeting him for the second time – just like meeting anyone for the second time – will only end up being a massive disappointment anyway. The ecstasy I felt last time will get replaced, as though by default, by awkwardness and tedious talk.

We should have left this exactly where we did – on a real high. That way I could be the happy owner of a beautiful memory, now and forever: one of the nicest evenings I ever had. And nothing would be able to destroy it.

Meeting him for the second time – just like meeting anyone for the second time – will only end up doing just that.

But my natural instinct is disabled, it seems; my natural instinct is pushing me in the other direction.

"Wish me luck."

"Luck? I think all I need to wish you is fun."

"Anyway, see you later."

"Or not."

She giggles into her tea. Apparently I'm not the only pubescent teenager in this flat.

I look at our mixed-up collection in the hallway. I still haven't decided which shoes to wear.

I look at myself in the narrow hallway mirror: My scarlet-coloured top has the thickness of a jumper, but no sleeves. The neck is low without being too revealing. I'm going for comfort, and therefore confidence, but not at anyone's expense, I think. The scarlet ends with my tight black jeans exactly. My brown hair is falling on my shoulders on either side.

My eyes, losing focus, blur my small silver earrings into the warning sign that keeps flashing. Frantically.

Everything I know about letting go is still with me. The personal journals I kept during the last ten years are bursting with telling experience, the same old tale: Either you heed the warning sign, or you'll end up making yourself vulnerable. Either you show some respect, or you'll end up putting yourself in a position I really don't want to put myself in.

I shake my head, shaking back my focus, but elsewhere in my body it's all up and down and up again, and there's nothing I can do.

In a part of myself that has been half-asleep for I-don't-know-how-long, the jumps are on, and I don't know how to ignore them.

Slippers, sneakers, boots. Heels? I hate the concept and I wouldn't even consider wearing the unused would-be pair I own if I didn't have a feeling he might like them. That's a ridiculous way to think: I get into the black slippers I wore last time.

One text – that's all that would be needed to cancel this night, cuddle up with the network, and breathe normally again. Why are you not sending it, I'm asking myself, hands on my hips, in the mirror. Why?

I rush out to catch the bus before I have a chance to answer.

12

The fourteenth floor could have been the end of it. During the days that followed the party, life went on as it does, now, that I have settled, at least for the foreseeable future: I took a bus to work; I took a bus from work.

But, for some reason, the specialist magazine on the international energy market that hired me as an editorial assistant within a week of my arrival in the city, wasn't a specialist magazine any longer. For me, the tiring talk on markets and opportunities that dominates our morning conference – the only time I actually come close to editorial issues; the rest of the time, my job title is more accurately that of a secretary – had never connected to real life, let alone my life.

Suddenly, every word spoken seemed to underline what had started to germinate inside of me.

For days, I stared at my computer screen, but instead of updating the editorial schedule, or making appointments for a group of oil company representatives, or sending out next week's feature list, I travelled.

I travelled, just the way we travelled, that night, standing next to each other behind the window, gazing at our city.

Grabbing a single light, I moved along inefficient, out-dated power lines, until I reached an inefficient, out-dated power station. I could make out waste wherever I looked, but my journey took me further, through the station's chimney, and into the air, where the smoke's everyday pollution didn't even register and then, finally, into the atmosphere – where the real harm is being done. Far away from us. Where no one is looking.

I travelled, again and again, until I was locked in, firmly – in the atmosphere – where it wasn't just my station, pushing up the planet's thermostat, of course, but thousands of other stations, and millions of cars, and hundreds of planes, too.

Up there, I realised what it was all these have in common: They all lead back down here, to us. They all lead back down here. To me. Sitting at my desk. Living my life.

That was the real difference. The place where this half-familiar journey began: right here. With me.

How could I have condemned this – the faulty system that powers just about everything we do, day after day, hour for hour – to such a marginalised and neglected existence for so long?

For days, the conflicts she presented to me that night were bouncing inside of me, but instead of unsettling me or turning me off – that was the real difference here – they charged me up and pushed me to pull up my sleeves and start the work to resolve them. To return some sort of balance. A new connection had started to emerge. Connecting me.

That's why it's not too hard to guess what my answer was, when I received this text in the dead afternoon hour of 3pm, sitting in front of my screen as we all sit in front of our screens in the dead afternoon hour of 3pm, having accepted the office-bound default in all its full-time monotony:

Bring your contradictions & your energy. Tonight at 8. Don't be shy. No one bites.

I came unprepared; that made everything possible. I know this now. Had I known even just a tiny bit more than that, I would have acted the way I have with those alternative after-work activities I considered at the time (yoga, singing lessons, knitting): I wouldn't have gone. As with all of those, the effort required – the getting used to strangers I wouldn't like, probably; the awkwardness of the first sessions – would have overshadowed the benefits and I would have decided that, on balance, it wasn't worth it.

Had I caught a glimpse of them before – of, say, the ex-banker's neatly pressed shirt, the fashionista's over-the-top lipstick, the brain's nerdy rims, the leader's fury face – my judgemental self might have said No too.

But I went. I didn't defend, refuse, reason. I simply let go and jumped in, and here I am, at the heart of this prototype, collaborating with a bunch of strangers who found each other in ways I still don't know about, doing something I still can't believe. I looked beyond the facade and found something much purer in these people. Something much richer.

The outcome of this experiment is anyone's guess. All I know is that I can't walk away from it anymore.

13

Behind the taxi's window on my side, neon-lit shop fronts are starting to become front doors, office towers tower blocks, central streets residential ones.

Cities – that's all those lives, touching and letting go again. Constantly. Touching, and letting go.

I turn away from my window. They are stories, I sometimes think, our cities. Stories we are writing together. No one, I think, has figured them out yet. No one can claim to say: This is the way it should be done. It's trial-and-error, all the time. The story is being written anew – every day, and every night, and I am writing a very special chapter tonight; we are. He and me.

Neither of us had to ask the question; neither of us had to give the answer.

The taxi driver doesn't see how his hand touches my knee and he doesn't see how I'm reaching out, pulling him towards me, but our noses must be right there, in his rear-view mirror, as they touch for the very first time. As we touch, he and me. For the very first time.

I can smell our wine in his breath, but not just that, and I can feel the nervousness that opens my mouth:

"Did you see the tree before we got in?"

"The tree?"

"Maybe it's just me noticing these things."

"I'm intrigued."

I know it's more than just nervousness. It's the green. These eyes are opening me up the way a key opens a door:

"It started in this city, I think. It could be a lonely flower in a front garden, a robin hopping on a fence, or a silly old shrub, but mainly, it's trees. Sometimes, I imagine these moments in succession. It's my latest trick to... You're the first one who's ever heard about this."

His hand is on my thigh now, warm through the jeans. I'm feeling the fabric of his shirt.

"It all started with my tree, in the garden of our flat. I can see it through the window when I'm lying in bed. I see its branches against whatever colour the sky takes: a rainy day grey, a day-after blue, the rose glow of a summer night, the white of a full moon."

"You have trouble sleeping?"

"Terrible, yes. Every night. If I look at the tree the right way, it ceases to be a tree and turns into something much more abstract, much closer to my heart. Its branches become part of a larger structure, like ways my mind might travel. Like decisions I made, routes I chose. I can't believe I'm telling you this."

"I'm very glad you do."

A red light tears us apart. I grab his shirt and, coming closer again, our lips don't wait for our permission.

He tastes sweet – sweeter than expected, and a little more male. Hungry, but tender.

His hand moves up my leg, holding my waist. My hand is inside his dark blond hair now.

Whatever was still talking inside of me finally shuts up. Against his tongue, the warning sign doesn't stand a chance.

For a short moment it's as though everything is falling away, the taxi we're sitting in and the street we're driving down and the city we're living in, and all the lights.

For a moment, it's as though there's no movement at all. I can't feel the departure and I don't long for the arrival. As his mouth gently encloses my lower lip, there is only this, the in-between. There's only the being, and it's beautiful.

"I've been dreaming about this. All week."

It's him, saying this, not me.

I have my hand on his cheek now, just below his ears, as though I'm holding him up – to see if he's for real.

Is this just another harmless evening, something he might be getting from someone else tomorrow night, or something that's just between him and me?

His breath strokes my face.

Is he acting like this because he can't help himself, or because he's trying to tell me something?

There are no answers to these questions, unarticulated, just like there were none on our table: Why is he so elusive about his professional plans? Why is it that he refuses to talk about his job for more than a minute? His relationship wishes – why is he even less forthcoming about these? Why does he avoid anything that might touch on this, even just remotely?

All night, the barrier between my brain and my mouth lay next to my wine glass – broken – and I'm still making sense of how that could have happened, but the same wasn't true at the table's other end, was it? And yet, our conversations never faltered: My feeble interest in cooking was stirred, curiously, by his chef-like passion for it; my love for fiction bounced off his stubborn commitment to fact. For an instant, the atheist in him teased out whatever seems to be hiding behind my comfortable agnosticism, before we turned where I steered us last time.

But this time it was him, leading us there, and I don't think he did so to make us get up.

I tried very hard not to mention the bare room to him: Nothing would be gained from that at all, I feel. In fact, nothing would be more counter-productive right now. Dangerous even.

I carefully talked about my latest passion, the Arctic – vaguely and philosophically. I told him: It's up there, beneath the receding ice, that our future is being decided. It's up there, in the depth of largely untouched waters, that we – as a civilisation – will be able to show that we have actually learnt something in the last few decades. I said: It's up there, where the earth keeps its last remaining mysteries, where the earth is still itself, that we will be able to show that there's some dignity left in us.

When his attitude – somewhere between cynical and resigned; I'm not sure where to put my finger – started to overwhelm me, I suggested another bottle of wine, and he smiled.

His hand is where the scarlet meets my skin now, his fingers amid my head's brown.

"I like your hair like that, by the way."

I'm sliding around his neck, pulling him towards me.

"But I saw it online anyway."

"So you did look?"

"Only the picture."

The picture that's giving away too much, my smile too broad, my nose too sharp and prominent.

"I don't blame you. I looked too. But neither of us clicked, and I'm glad."

He's too serious on his, annoyingly business-like. The moment I saw it, I clicked away, not to destroy my picture of him – the picture that's in my hands now.

"When it really counts, the network is so counter-productive, isn't it? Are you there often?"

"All the magic, taken by a click, yes. I'm there too often. It's a little..."

"Sad?"

"Don't tease me. Are you there often?"

"No."

"You're so straightforward, aren't you?"

"Not nearly as straightforward as you think."

"What should I think?"

"What do you want to think?"

That these eyes mean more than anyone's eyes have ever meant. That these lips are true. That there's more to this face, this laugh and this voice, so much more. That maybe – just maybe – I'm prepared to go one small step further than I have done in years.

"Don't."

I trap his finger between my shoulder and my chin.

"I'm so ticklish there."

"Don't you allow me to tickle you a little?"

I feel him on my back now.

"If you keep looking like that, I'm going to allow you to do pretty much anything in a minute."

14

What chance do I have if this can hit me on a night like tonight? In such a moment.

The unease I get whenever I think of my junction has become normal, almost. The feeling that the things I have done with my life so far are having real consequences, for the first time; and that my options are running out – I can handle that, just the way I can handle the dreadful sense that, sometimes, I can't converse with anyone, anymore, because the complex code that comes with a life lived firmly in one environment is alien to me now.

But this is very different. This attacks me – the way it just has – out of nowhere, but it doesn't hit from somewhere outside; it hits from within.

And it's not possible to run away from something that hits from within.

I shudder. No one told me this would be the result; no one warned me. At no point during the last ten years did anyone dare to point my head – always slightly raised, always looking ahead – at the ground. There, at the ground, the layers must have been piling, then already.

I've peeled myself; that's how far I've come in my analysis. With every city, another layer has come off. With every country, I lost another skin. And I had no idea.

Another opportunity, a new job, a mere feeling – people like me don't need to be pushed; people like me need to be held back, restrained, chained, but no one did that for me, and so I grabbed what I could grab, and no one predicted that I would reach something I still don't understand this way. Something I can't even name. Something I haven't noticed before. Something I can't really grasp.

It's deep inside of me; that's all I know. It's raw. And it scares me. It really, really scares me.

15

"Of course you waited until after you've fucked me to tell me this."

The vague shine of a candle flickers over our bodies. His chest is warm against my small breasts. Uncovered, our legs are entangled, our naked tummies touching.

"It's not like that. Honestly. There just wasn't... I'm sorry."

"No... Yes... I mean: no."

"I should have told you last time."

"You should have, yes, I mean, given it happened so recently."

"Yes."

But then, isn't the fact that he didn't a much stronger signal, the one I actually prefer?

"How did it end?"

"How did it end, yes."

"What does that mean?"

"That means it's a little hard to say."

"Okay?"

Is it foolish of me to think that if he had the decency not to poison either of our tables with love gone wrong, how much clearer could he be about sensing what I sensed then, what I sensed all evening, what I'm sensing now?

"Our love... I guess, it just stopped."

"Your love just stopped?"

"That's the best way I can describe it."

"How long were you going out?"

"Quite some time."

"Did you cheat? Did she?"

"No, nothing happened at all. It just stopped. Just like that. It was the weirdest experience."

"And so you split, no hurt feelings?"

"Not exactly."

"Do you still talk?"

"Not much, no."

"But, I mean, didn't you try to work it out? Well, I'm not the one to talk really..."

"It didn't work, nothing did. I have never felt like that before. It destroyed everything I used to believe about love and relationships. It all... I don't know... It left me quite disillusioned."

"Quite a bit of disillusionment going on that end, isn't there? So, are you still thinking of her?"

"No."

"You're sure?"

"Yes. But let's not talk about it, okay? It's over. It really is. I'm sorry I didn't tell you."

His lips, by way of underlining this, make their way from my collarbone, slowly up my neck, over my chin.

It could have been easier, of course – she, having run away with another man, having moved to another country, gone for good. But it could have been much harder too – she having told him that she merely needed some time, leaving him still attached, longing, in love. This is a modern day muddle, neither here, nor there. And if there's anything I know how to handle, it's that, right?

The way our tongues meet feels almost familiar. His fingers slide down my side on a wave of gooseflesh.

The sex was a disaster, of course. He didn't get hard at first, citing nervousness, the usual; my hands just got sweatier and sweatier. The condom we both insisted on didn't help, and neither did the cold in the room, his heating turned off at night, naturally.

Words have the power, though: It's so nice to be with you, I whispered and that's when he rose. Just don't stop holding me, I whispered, and that's when he entered me.

It's no secret – my journeys did their job fulfilling my sexual desires. The last ten years satisfied my curiosity; my storage of bedroom experience has been loaded to the full.

But half an hour ago wasn't just sex, the way adults play. Once he was where I wanted him, we handed ourselves over – unasked, not under anyone's control – and as a result, our shared movement was slower than most I can remember, and deeper. And not just in a physical sense.

"You know, I was really interested in what we talked about earlier. And last time, at the end."

"Really?"

I grab the blanket from the bottom of the bed and cover both of us without asking.

"I just introduced it last time to… never mind. I don't understand. It's about your work, isn't it?"

Our heads are next to each other on his pillow now.

"It's not really about work."

"Some would disagree, yes."

"Who would disagree?"

"Oh, no one, nothing…"

"Nothing? You looked quite… I don't know, disturbed there, for a second."

"Well, some friends."

"You talked to them about me?"

"No… Yes, sorry. Yes, they asked me about you and I told them about your work and it interested them, because… they're interested."

"I see."

"Are they close friends?"

"Close friends? I'm not sure. I'm sort one of them, if you like... Anyway, let's not –"

"One of them? Sounds like some sort of a gang."

"Well, it sort of is."

"Really? I'm intrigued."

"Sounds intriguing, I know. It's nothing special, though. We're just a bunch of people, meeting, talking."

"Just talking."

"About ways out, yes. About ways forward."

"Sounds great. How is it going?"

"Hey, I thought you didn't want to talk about work."

"It's not work."

"Don't you know the answer yourself?"

"Well, I guess I can imagine."

"If you're interested, I can take you there one day, but I don't think now's the time to talk about it."

"Would you?"

"What?"

"Take me there?"

"Well, yes…"

"I'd be very interested. I mean, I told you I –"

I replace my index finger with a kiss that's so long and strong it kicks our conversation right out of bed. Not to return. He emerges from it with a silent smile.

In the half-light, his features look even prettier.

I keep looking into the silence that's starting to engulf our naked bodies, as though it was an embrace. I know that if I was alone now, in my own bed, something would be crawling into it without mercy, quietly covering more and more of my peeled result in a pitiless black...

Sometimes, when it stretches really badly, nothing helps, not picking up the novel that used to excite me a few days ago, not the song I once loved, not a glass of wine and not three glasses of wine either. Sometimes, I manage to save myself by committing whatever triggered the attack to paper, by admitting defeat in writing, at least, but a temporary fix isn't what I'm graving for tonight.

Tonight, I'm longing for something a little more permanent, a little more flesh and blood.

I place my hand on his naked chest. His fingers, when he does the same, feel right on me, so right.

He smiles:

"I can feel what's beating inside of you."

"So can I."

I let my other hand slide down his back, halting where the small of it stops being the small of it, and pull him towards me. His hand, moving sideways a little, brushes my breast, and then I'm in his arms, and yet he is in mine.

"What are you thinking?"

In those green eyes, I'm thinking, I can just be – but my answer is just for me.

I let my hand slide a little further down, stroking what's firm beneath the softness of his skin. His hand remains where I want it to be, so close to where no attack has a chance as a result.

How beautifully you're filling *this*, I'm thinking. How perfectly you fit in, right here. As though tailor-made. As though made just for me. I'm thinking: You.

I turn my head away, hoping for the room's darkness to swallow my smile:

Am I really prepared to believe that, this time round, the promise is real?

Two

Chosen Regime

It's one of my iron rules, freedom where freedom is due. It seems to be one of his iron rules too: One week has passed since we talked and kissed until Sunday fell through his blinds. One week without him.

Through it, fragments of our all-night conversation kept coming back to me, almost every day. Sentence for sentence, it seemed, only the right words were coming out of my mouth that night – without me doing much.

Even sitting in his kitchen, after a few hours of sleep, dishevelled in his washed-out white T-shirt, slurping muesli with orange juice, because the milk was out, I managed to keep my control freak underneath the table. It's so nice to spend time with you, he said.

I would have stayed for lunch and dinner and another night in his bed. Easily. But he had to prepare some very important things for work, he said, the moment we had finished the coffee, leaving my nosy question unanswered: What is it you have to prepare?

I understood, of course: *I* used to be the one who was desperate for breathing space after a night with someone. I changed back into my own clothes, and kissed him goodbye, softly and quickly, on his doorstep. When I turned around, several steps down the street he's living on, he was waving at me.

At that moment, I felt, his entire body was filled with a longing.

It's this image – so vivid and strong – which has provided the starting point for every route my aroused imagination has taken me on this week, whirling me up higher, and higher still – in the bus to work, in the bus from work, at work and in bed, twisting and turning. Every single night.

One week – and neither of us dared to go beyond a text. Our excited back-and-forth stayed unbroken, but neither of us managed to break out.

Nineteen messages; I counted them this morning, and every single one of them is filled with beauty. With *his* beauty. Every sentence in them seems carefully crafted, each x filled with meaning. There is so much tenderness in those words, and so much respect for me, and yet: Not one suggested a follow-up in the real world. Not a bed, not a table-for-two, not even a drink. *Sweet dreams to you.*

One week – or, to be precise: six days. Tomorrow – Saturday – would have made it one week.

But instead:

"We heard you're a politician."

"Well, not quite, I'm –"

"Come in."

"I'm a politician's assistant, but I'm more interested to hear what you guys are up to in here."

"I bet you are."

I close the door behind us.

"But we are all rather interested in what you are up to in your job. Or not up to, for that matter."

Our leader has her hands propped up on her waist. From her red curls down to her mock-Converse, her entire body is demanding answers, answers, answers from him.

The brain, the fashionista and the ex-banker – all of them seated – are nodding.

"Look, I know it must be somewhat frustrating –"

"Somewhat frustrating? Did you hear that guys? Somewhat frustrating."

A terrible mistake, this. I was standing on the small balcony we have at work when he finally called, earlier today. It's being used by smokers, mainly, but it's looking out onto a small tree, so it's being used by me too. When he said that, sadly, the weekend would be extremely busy the way this week has been, I saw myself, twisting and turning in the shadow of my tree, being tortured for two nights in a row.

That's when I carefully mentioned the meeting tonight. He said Yes before I had even finished the sentence.

"She's right. Everything out there has moved on in the last few months – except you."

That from the fashionista. She's in dark jeans and a red/white/red T-shirt. Her wavy black hair is bound together tightly today. It's a conservative look for her standards. Her slippers are lying in front her, as though she no longer wants them.

"I think you must have a certain degree of sympathy for politicians. It's –"

"Do we really?"

I know how long our leader has waited for something like this to happen; I know how hungry she is.

"It's not always as straight-forward as it looks from the outside."

The surprising calm in every word he has uttered so far would have disarmed many an opponent. Not this gang, though.

"A complete and utter lack of ambition when it comes to the most pressing issue we're facing – sounds very straightforward to me. How about you guys?"

They're all nodding; the three of them are merely supporting her assault. The centre of the stage is hers.

I'm just standing here, staring a hole into my regret.

"There. Just out today."

She points at the perfectly bound pile of A4 that's lying on the brain's lap.

"Another comprehensive study, co-produced by a group of leading international engineers and a coalition of the world's major environmental organisations."

The brain:

"Which shows that close to a hundred percent renewable energy by 2050 is feasible – if the right decisions are taken *right now*."

"As for the likes of you – you're looking into it. You're fucking looking into it as you have done for – you, tell, me, for how many years now?"

"I know."

"Well, great you do."

I wonder if he exchanged his shirt for a plain T-shirt to meet us on our level, whether they are taught such things in politics school. Though what I'm really thinking is that I like him in a plain T-shirt as much as I like him in a shirt, if not more.

"What you have to understand is how much there's at work that limits our ability to manoeuvre."

The confidence!

"Any decision taken here affects and is affected by so many other decisions elsewhere. It's a constant struggle, internally. For resources. For attention."

The composure!

"I can assure you that any environmental department anywhere in the world is probably filled with plenty of people who have the right intentions and are trying really hard. But you have to take into account what they're up against."

The credibility!

"If this, or the environment in general, was the only topic on the agenda, we might have cracked it by now. Unfortunately it isn't. People are demanding things from from all sides. Equally justified things. Equally important things. And they are screaming just as loud as you are. I can tell you that."

The control!

"And all too often these things stand in direct competition or conflict with what you're asking."

His words cut through our anger like a sharp knife.

I look at the others.

The brain's facial expression has changed, almost completely. It's as though he's switched sides:

"I understand."

"Oh, do you?"

The leader takes a step away from him. The fashionista:

"Let the boss deal with it."

But the brain doesn't respond. Was everything I ever said or did in this room in error? That's how he looks.

"One for the elites, this."

If it's that easy for the fashionista to slip into protective irony, why doesn't it happen to her much more often, I wonder. The leader stamps her foot on the ground:

"No one's elite in here!"

The word enrages her; anything in that vein does, I've come to realise.

"Whatever."

The fashionista waves her off. The ex-banker is surprisingly quiet today. He's looking up from a chair he has turned around, his arms on its rest, his chin on his arms. He's looking strangely in awe. Strangely softened. How much tenderness is there, I wonder, inside his shell?

Looking at our group like that, I'm being reminded of how little I know them, still. I can feel each and every one of them so intensely, and yet: gaps are gaps, and some of them are secrets. What isn't being asked about, has to reveal itself voluntarily, and it's a process that can't be rushed; it can only be tickled, every now and then.

"What the likes of you still don't get is this: We're not talking about the environment any longer!"

She pushes up the sleeves of her jumper:

"You know, as if it was merely one of many issues."

"Unfortunately it is."

"Unfortunately it isn't, but the likes of you just don't get it, do you?"

"Right, so what *are* you talking about?"

"Our place on the planet. The way we do things. And how we will do things in the future. We're talking about... everything."

She crosses her arms. As though to present her breasts, I sneer to myself.

He takes a deep breath:

"But in reality, what you're saying comes down to specific topics, issues, aspects. You can't just be talking about everything. If you actually want to act, rather than to just talk, you have to break things down into things you can actually tackle. That's what we're doing in government. And that's when it gets complicated and dirty."

The brain nods. The fashionista has switched off. Our feisty leader is unimpressed:

"But you're not even acknowledging the bigger picture. Let's at least start to talk about what inaction will mean for all of us. I still have to hear a politician make that point."

This is exactly why I wanted to prevent this. I remember my first meetings. I know how I struggled to understand what, exactly, made the others so angry, what fired them up in a way I hadn't seen – anywhere.

It took me a while to see the direct line they had established between themselves and the world's inaction; it was as though every minute that passed without change racked up their agitation, without them even doing anything:

"I still have to see any kind of understanding of the scale of what's actually going on right now. That's the whole problem: You're still not telling it as it is, are you?"

"I'm... I'm aware of that. But... we have no choice, sometimes."

She has her hands on her hips again:

"Yes you do. You always have a choice. But you prefer to pretend that everything will just go away. Or that someone else is going to sort it out for you."

Her voice has lost none of its anger, or its strength, but there's something else in there now, something that's much harder to define, because it's softer, somehow:

"You're waiting for the day when it's going to be one hundred percent safe to speak out on this to your electorate – the day when things are going to be so blindingly obvious that not even the tiniest minority of the electorate will be able to have a grudge against you. That's when you will act."

He's looking down now.

"But let me break it to you, mister politician-I'm-not-really-a-politician..."

He doesn't look up.

"…when that day comes, it will be too late."

A dreadful silence fills the room.

It's too much to bear. I can't see him suffer like that. I take a step forward:

"There have been some promising small steps, of course."

"Give me a break, small steps."

My cheeks are saying hello and I'm regretting my words already – probably because I didn't really mean them. Our leader is shaking her head:

"As long as people like him keep using their baby walk as an excuse for not making the real leap, the one we actually need, we're not getting anywhere. We all know that."

He's still looking down:

"What I have tried to explain is that in politics, all too often, small steps is all you are able to take."

"Yes, and what I've tried to explain is that that's just not good enough anymore."

"Right then, so what *is* it that you want?"

2

The impossible; we know that. We want something so incredibly bold and beautiful it dizzies me every time I think about it. The Great Turnaround, the fashionista said a few weeks ago, and twisted, like a beautiful ballerina. Let's call it the Great Turnaround.

It's positively mad; we know that too. We believe that humanity will stop mid-run. Not because there's a wall. Not because there's a hill. Not because there's even the slightest obstacle preventing us from going on exactly the way we're going right now – simply because we decide to.

We believe that humanity will pull off the boldest U-turn God, or whoever is looking down on us, has ever seen. Not asked by a government. Not pushed by so-called market forces, or another religion. Simply because we understand.

We're imagining the unimaginable: For us to shun what's running out and heating us – *before* it does either for real.

For us to stop the digging, the scraping, the drilling and the fracking *before* we have to – and leave in the ground what we can't safely burn anymore, anyway.

For us to reclaim the steering wheel we surrendered – to whom exactly? – and change course, collectively. That's what we want.

3

"Come on. Don't pretend you don't know how our cute little system works."

The sarcastic laugh that accompanies this statement is the ex-banker's. He's shaking his head at our visitor.

The three of them – the two men and our leader – are standing in the middle of the room now. The fashionista has done with the brain what I would love to do with him: Take his hand and drag him. Out. Of. Here.

But he hasn't looked at me – not once.

"Don't you agree? Companies should play their part, shouldn't they?"

And now something is happening that doesn't allow me to walk away, even though I'm still making sense of it. Is it in the way they stand? Like a triangle.

"Of course they should. Unfortunately, we also require them to place profit above pretty much everything else, and for that reason alone, they can't consider this to the extend we need them to right now. I used to work in mergers and acquisitions, you see."

"Right."

"Unless it's in their economic interest to move, they won't. Which brings us back to you lot."

He points his finger at our visitor, but our visitor points at our leader:

"And what about people? Don't we all have to make drastic changes to our lifestyle if we want to get anywhere?"

"Of course we do, and we are. More people are getting into the reduced lifestyle by the day. But we will only go one step further if companies and governments help us."

She points at both of them.

"And yet companies will not do anything if they don't get strong signals from both people and governments."

The ex-banker points at our visitor and our leader.

"And still, only politicians can set limits, impose standards, channel the money where it needs to go."

She points back at our visitor.

"And yet, we can't allow our competitiveness to suffer. Make all the vague talk specific and what you get is: People need jobs, whatever these jobs are."

At the leader.

"And that means companies, whatever they make."

At the ex-banker.

"And whatever gets damaged, often irreversibly. And we politicians need to make sure it's happening."

My eyes open a little wider. For a moment, it seems as though the scene in front of me is frozen in time: the three of them, all pointing at one another, feverishly.

"That's just the way things work."

In our chosen regime – the term just floods at me, out of nowhere. I hold on to every letter.

"And every politician out there knows it."

For a moment, it seems as though I'm removed from the scene. In my head, the three of them are forming a triangle: I see politicians; I see companies; I see the people. And I see their fingers, pointing, feverishly.

The set-up we have created, I realise, doesn't just allow for it; the set-up we created asks for it.

The chosen regime – is this who we surrendered the steering wheel to?

The three of them stand unmoved, as though they're unsure what to say next. The ex-banker slides his hands into his back pockets, she has hers entangled upfront, in semi-defeat. Our visitor lets both his arms drop:

"Anyway, there's still so much uncertainty about the technology we will need, about the complicated new grid we will need to build. How do we guarantee supply? How do we convince people to pay more for their electricity? How do we make them accept windmills in their backyards? There is just so much that hasn't been answered when it comes to the feasibility of it all."

I can't believe he's giving us this worn-out drivel, but his voice prevents me from exposing it.

"Let's face it, to commit to the kind of redesign you're advocating in here – you know, a real re-design, not just some cosmetic changes here and there, not just the kind of panic reaction we saw after Fukushima to please our electorates – that still amounts to the biggest risk any politician has taken. Anywhere. And probably ever."

Our leader:

"Of course it does. Have we said it's going to be easy?"

"No."

"Have we said there isn't going to be a risk involved?"

"No."

"What we're saying is: You need to take the risk. But if you went into politics to smile on talk shows, then I don't know."

"I can assure you I didn't go into politics to smile on talk shows. I went into politics to... Whatever."

Maybe it's the phrase, which continues to overlay everything that's happening in front of me, or maybe it's the childish way I just jumped to his defence again, or maybe it's the fact that I gave up all hope it would happen, but when he finally looks at me, I don't hear, at first, what he's saying.

"Will you?"

"Will I what?"

"Take me out. I feel exhausted. It's been great meeting you all, but it's quite hard work to, you know... Anyway."

"Sure."

"Why is it? Tell me."

She doesn't want to let go. He turns:

"Why is what?"

"Why is it that an entire generation of politicians around the world has discarded political courage as if that was the prerequisite for becoming a politician in the first place – why, why, why?"

"Let's go, okay?"

As the door falls shut behind us, I realise I haven't even said goodbye to them.

The air smells foul in the narrow corridor that leads away from the bare room. The floor creaks. I take his hand and start leading him, carefully, through the darkness.

There's no question: He was taken by her passion, just as she was in awe of his cool command. The way he handled her anger spurred our leader in a whole new way, and her face didn't conceal the confirmation she got out of it. It seemed to please her more than confirmation from any of us ever has. There's no question the others were affected too. His charisma doesn't just work on me, that's for sure.

But I can't help feeling that something bigger has happened in there, and one part of me wants to rewind immediately and find an excuse not to introduce him to the group. Any excuse! Because it's evidently not a good idea.

Another part of me tells me something else, but I don't really understand that part.

I need to see the group again – without him, on Monday – to find out either way, but for now, this ordeal is over and I'm already imagining him, holding me the way he held me last week, my head against his naked chest, strangely at ease. Strangely at peace.

I'm already imagining me, gently supporting his head. It's what draws me to him more than anything, I think, the way we meet each other as equals. How we're eye to eye. There's a beautiful balance of power, a perfect equilibrium of control. The bare room's intensity might have unsettled it a little, too many forces pulling too many strings, but now that we're approaching neutral territory, it can all come back. Now, it's just the two of us again. He stops; I turn.

There's just enough light in here for his face to be half-lit. The shine is splitting him.

"Can I come to a meeting again? It was quite…"

"We'll see. Let's not –"

"You don't want me to?"

"What do you want to do now, is my question. Let's see if we find a place around here, what do you think?"

Whatever happened in-between those walls, I have no interest in a replay.

"I'm quite tired, to be honest."

"Okay, do you want to…"

"I think I'd like to go home, actually."

"What do you mean?"

A non-telling shine wraps his face. I can't read what I'm seeing; I don't understand what I just heard.

"Is that okay?"

His face moves backwards, further into the dark, away from me. I don't respond.

I see. Having imposed his reality check on a bunch of unsuspecting dreamers, the voice of reason needs a rest, is that it? Having been stimulated like that by the bare room, our visitor is quite content. Correct?

Having taken whatever he wanted to take from inside there – that's it for now. Is that it?

4

"Not spending Friday night with your new man?"

"My new man, yes."

"Not going well?"

"I wouldn't say that."

"So?"

I hang my black cotton bag on the rest of a chair in front of me and lean onto it.

My two flatmates are both sitting at our kitchen table, each of them with a bowl of pasta, both chewing. The clock above them tells me that it's much later than I thought it was. The empty pot standing on the sink tells me that they didn't expect me for dinner anyway. There's a bottle of wine in-between them.

My outspoken flatmate is still looking at me, probingly, but the electrifying thoughts I had on my way here – wouldn't the Great

Turnaround be a spectacular return of our collective willpower? – were so effective in keeping *my new man* at bay, I'm struggling to do the same to them now.

"Glass of wine? You look like you need one, to be honest. Here. There's some left in our bottle."

All the way here, real meaning kept striking down the outside's distorted perceptions, its wicked preconceptions, the destructive hiss of cynicism. Inside of me, a vision was able to flourish, and it flourished beautifully.

My quiet flatmate is pointing at the glass she has filled for me. It's standing on the table in-between them.

The threshold of respectability, the categories of what's called right-thinking, the supposedly proper interpretation – I ignored them all for my thoughts to cross the border we have drawn for ourselves and, inside of me, become much purer. Much truer.

And I really don't care if my words sound terribly over-the-top: the schmaltzy meanderings of a madhouse. I allowed my flow to happen despite of it; I allowed my flow to happen because of it:

"Hey, I just had some amazing thoughts on –"

"Oh, spare us, please."

"Yes – not interested, thanks a lot."

"Hey, I haven't even…"

"No, but your voice is giving you away. Honestly, I had a very stressful day at work and I'm trying to relax, okay? Because, hurray, tomorrow's going to be just as stressful. And whatever you guys are getting up to in that dark room of yours – it's not going to be very relaxing, is it?"

My outspoken flatmate is twisting her dark brown curls the way she usually does when speaking.

Her legs are crossed, tensely, her feet still in their heels. Her light blue blouse stretches, as she places her empty bowl onto the table:

"Sorry we didn't leave you any pasta, by the way."

Her quiet counterpart is wearing a red T-shirt that's in a stark contrast to her shortly-cut blonde hair.

The two of them couldn't be much more different from each other, really – the outspoken one tall, curvy and brash; the quiet one small, slim and inconspicuous – but I can't imagine them apart. Probably because I've only ever known them together.

"No worries, I'm not hungry, but I can't understand why you're not even listening, for once."

"Because we have a lot of other things to worry about. No offence, but out here, you know, it's normal life. I have hard days at work and I have a right to relax in the evening."

She gets up with her bowl and puts it into the sink in one swift move.

"Anyway, there's enough people interested already, isn't there? People with more time. People with nothing else to do. There's no need for two stressed professional women to add even more stress to their life, is there?"

"We need everyone."

Her hands are propped up where the light blue meets the beige of her trousers:

"Let me be perfectly honest with you, okay? Your getting on my nerves. I mean, your... thing is. I'm tired of being told by people like you how I'm supposed to live my life, okay? I have other issues... more important issues."

"But..."

"I don't need anyone preaching to me like that. As if you guys have all the wisdom in the world."

"She's right. I mean, do we really have to burden ourselves with all this, just because of some half-proven idea that this planet might be getting a little warmer in a hundred years or so?"

My quiet flatmate is leaning back, hands crossed in front of her flat chest, using her second favourite tone after motherly: sceptical.

"Exactly. It's getting a bit hotter. Whatever. I mean, let's just live."

"Enjoy your wine then."

I grab my bag and turn. The door to my room falls shut behind me with a bang that wasn't intended.

Why am I still not able to stand up to them? After everything I have learned and processed and done in the last two months, why am I still not able to even just explain. Why do I still not have the right words?

Or are those the wrong questions and the one I should be asking is this: Why do I still lack the courage?

I walk, without switching on the light, towards my bed. I drop my bag, and then myself.

Every time this happens, I tell myself that next time I will at least try to take some of the bare room's magic, and spread it in our kitchen.

If only I could show them – even for just as few seconds – what it's like on the other side. How exhilarating it can be, over there, where we believe in us, in all of us. If only there was a way for them to experience what I experienced before I entered our flat – for just a few seconds. For a mere glimpse. It could make all the difference, I think.

But today the opposite is happening, and I shouldn't be surprised.

I use my feet to take off my sneakers. They fall onto the floor at the bed's bottom, one, two.

Sometimes, a sentence is enough – a casual conversation, like the one that just happened between me and my flatmates. That's when I feel how the raw power drains from my vision, leaving only the enormity, leaving only the murderous challenge we're facing over this. That's when I feel how everything that was so overwhelming half an hour ago wrinkles, like a balloon. *I mean let's just live.*

And once I'm here, I'm vulnerable: What if my flatmates are right? What if everything is half as bad, after all? What if things are basically *okay*?

I roll over, lift my blanket, and roll back underneath, covering my jeans and half my jumper without unfolding it fully. Don't I have other issues too? Personal issues. More important issues.

Once I'm here, it doesn't take much for the poison to enter: What's the point burdening ourselves like that? *Out here, you know, it's just normal life.* Why shouldn't we just go on the way we do? When that's just fine? When that's what's going to happen in any case!

Gone – the road I could see half an hour ago has disappeared, completely. Now, there's nothing I can do to stop the sentence as it runs me over, a high-speed train of remonstration: There's no need for the kind of fuss we're trying to make.

I'm slipping down the wrong side of the wall and there's nothing I can do, but think of him again.

I throw away the blanket and rush up.

5

The wall – it's like that: Our belief in the impossible has a very mean neighbour, its complete loss.

The wall separates you from your hopeful self. It rises between the cynic and the person that was so good at imagining the unimaginable. When the ambition is gigantic the way ours is, things are fragile like that.

And unfair too. To slip down on the wrong side of the wall, the way I just did, is the easiest thing in the world, to climb back up: the hardest.

But at least I know where to go now: here. I'm staring at the text I have composed: Will you let me know when things are less busy?

It's only one click away from being sent, but it has been for more than an hour now.

I look up; I found this magical place only a few days ago, on a post-work walk around the edges of my neighbourhood. There's a bench and a tree and nothing else. A gust from below reminds me that it's still only April, still colder than expected at night. Almost tenderly, it plays with my fringe, ruffling it, as though that was its sole intention.

Coming up here feels like being elevated from the streets, where everything is blocked by people, choked by fumes; where you're perspective is always just the perspective of what you're seeing in that moment; where drifting into dreams is being discouraged by everything that surrounds you. Where none of what has started to happen up here would be possible.

Wish you were here – shouldn't that be my text?

I let my phone sink into my lap, holding down my finger to delete the words I've written, until there's nothing left but an empty message – once again.

It's a clear night. The lights are sharp against the sky's black: grater-like stacks of white, scattered reds, and all sorts of oranges, sprawling into the distance. I can only imagine the neon that's illuminating the streets, or the dim shine of a street lamp; a thousand headlights, snaking elsewhere, or a nervous blue, crossing dark neighbourhoods.

I try to relax my shoulders. Down there, it spreads, street for street. Junction for junction, neighbourhood for neighbourhood, the city I have decided to settle in, at least for the foreseeable future – and yet what I see is more. And yet, what I see is less.

It's simple, really: Finding a spot like this was always one of the first steps in any new city, a prerequisite, almost, for feeling at home. In some places I had to go out of my way to discover it, entering districts I had been actively discouraged from entering, braving the samey streets of suburbia, taking trains I had never taken, or narrow alleyways I felt I shouldn't. Elsewhere, it was so obvious every tourist guide mentioned it. Sometimes, hill wasn't really the right expression; at other times, no word hit it better.

Invariably, these hills gave me what few places in a city have to offer – a sense of perspective; a glimpse of the beyond – and now, they're all with me, these hills.

Now, that I found this one. That's the secret to what has started to happen up here: What I see is a character without a face. Everything as nothing. What I see is less a city than a canvas, and while this realisation shocked me to the bone the first time I came up here, it couldn't please me more – now, that I grasp the potential. Now, that I know what it's like.

I take a deep breath, and it happens almost immediately. In front of me, the lights begin to blur. The heavy drone that comes with our individualised mobility acquires hypnotic qualities. The canvas brightens, and on it, the picture is coming on.

Outlines are acquiring focus. Everything is sharpening itself. All the details are finding their places. It's happening just the way I was hoping it would – after my slip.

The drone has faded, almost completely. I can make out human voices, even from up here. The lights are no longer a sprawling blanket, but scattered, sparsely. It's as though every single one has reclaimed a special status, its real worth. The air has cleared, notably… My construct is waking up.

And with it the muddled look he gave me in the tunnel and the non-specific agreement we left each other with and the feeling I didn't expect – and can't stand – make way for another expedition that will yield plenty to take, I hope, when I see them again on Monday, and I can't wait for it.

In front of me, my picture has come on: I'm seeing what I've started to see… from here.

6

"What are *you* doing in here?"

He looks at me as though that was the most ridiculous question to ask. I close the door behind me.

I can't believe this: It's Monday evening. All weekend, this man didn't manage to press his Send button even just once, and yet here he is? All weekend, I didn't manage to press *my* Send button even just once, because I was heeding the warning sign, waiting and hoping, twisting and turning– and now this?

I take a step into the room. They are all looking at me.

"Come on in. We're talking money."

Like a cheese cake, our leader.

"Oh, are you? How great. I might even participate. If I'm allowed to."

They have never heard me speak like this. I can see the surprise on the fashionista's face, and on the brain's. They are both leaning against the back wall, facing the door.

The ex-banker has placed his shiny boots on our wooden table, laissez-faire executive-style:

"Your boyfriend just informed us that it's all down to money, in the end. Haven't got any left, the poor little ones."

He puts his hands behind his head and stretches. The smugness seems to flow from his gelled hair all the way to his toes.

"He's not my boyfriend."

I cross my arms.

"It's nice to see you."

His voice!

He's sitting opposite her, his legs straight, his hands in his lap. Perfectly disarming, annoyingly charming. What is it that he wants from us? Out of us. I really wonder.

"Overspent ourselves propping up the banks, have we? Remember all those zeros? All those goddamn zeros?"

"That was an emergency."

"Hell yeah, it was – and much obliged too."

If the ex-banker's grin grows any bigger than this he will fall off his chair, or explode:

"I can't really say that my former colleagues are quite as grateful, or that they've stopped doing any of what they used to do, but hey, thanks for keeping the show on the road. And for turning a blind eye on the tents too."

"So the banks were an emergency? Alright. They probably were. The money came from nowhere. Suddenly it was there. Well, what the fuck is this then?"

"They think I'm one crazy idiot, by the way, for having left the party half way, but, you know."

"Saying that we can't afford this is like saying we can't afford making our future okay for everyone, not just a few. And maybe it's true. Maybe we can't. Maybe you're right. Maybe we really gave it all to desperado-types like him..."

The ex-banker raises his hands, mocking innocence. She lets her index finger sink again.

"...and now there's nothing left for the rest of us. Real shame. Awfully sorry."

He's suffering, but this time round I don't care. I'm not sure whether that's in my voice or not, or what is:

"Depressing, isn't it? Hundreds of years of so-called human progress, and we're still not able to think just a few years ahead."

"What do you mean?"

I grab the chair that's empty next to the ex-banker and sit. It's still me who is a part of this group:

"I mean, we're surprised by a supposedly life-threatening situation like the banks –"

"Which was merely a way-of-life-threatening situation, really."

The brain, from the back. I nod at him, approvingly.

"And we're suddenly able to do all these really big things. How hard can it be to use our brains and take just one step ahead, and realise what a life-threatening situation we are facing right now? Not for the planet. To say that is stupid. The planet's going to survive, don't you worry. But for so many people out there."

"And, again, the wrong people."

It's a point close to the fashionista's heart. But not just to hers.

"Yes."

Our leader rushes up:

"Yes? That's all you got to say? Yes?"

The fashionista pushes her down from behind:

"Relax."

He turns to me and his eyes are: The last thing I want is for you to be upset with me. And I wish I wasn't.

How many times have I been on the other side of this? How many times was it me, not playing ball? How many times – erratic, unreliable, selfish! You behaved like him a hundred times, girl, a hundred times worse.

He's putting a little distance between those intense first encounters and whatever will come next. I shouldn't over-interpret what shouldn't be over-interpreted. I have no grounds for accusations, not even for being disgruntled, really.

But I am. All of the above. And worse. Everything that is happening is happening on a new level and I'm unsure what to do, what to say, how to handle anything.

Staring into nowhere, I hear, vaguely, how the collapse of the banking system is going to be a joke compared to what's about to go down if. I hear about millions of people in dozens of countries. About fragile ecosystems and the complex construct we call nature.

His voice brings me back:

"Right, so here's my question for you."

He gets up from his chair.

Five pair of eyes are looking up to the very man I dreamt of having next to me all weekend.

"Here's the question I wanted to ask you from the first moment."

Stroking me and kissing me and holding me.

"What are you going to do about it?"

"What do you mean?"

"Well, politicians in the current set up won't move or, in any case, won't move fast enough. Consensus?"

"Indeed."

"Well, how will you make them move?"

It's as though the silence has fallen out of everyone's mouths, has sunken to the floor and is now rising up the walls again, filling the room in its entirety, paralysing everyone.

No one says a word.

I can hear the ex-banker's watch, ticking away seconds. I can hear myself thinking: Please don't.

But the ex-banker has already taken down his boots:

"Well."

I don't even know how we got to this point. How we slithered into this radical terrain, almost by accident.

"Well?"

Let's talk about voluntary carbon reduction schemes! Or about the positive impact government-sponsored forest protection schemes could have. Let's talk about anything, but this.

Please. He shouldn't be hearing this!

"We have been doing the things we have been doing for months, haven't we?"

The ex-banker's voice is unusually calm. There's not a hint of smugness left:

"What has changed? Exactly."

Let's talk about that thorniest of all issues, growth! Just the way we did last time, when we were at each other's throat over de-coupling, and all claims cancelled each other out.

"Things have come to a standstill. Absolute standstill. Which is to say: Nothing is fucking happening."

International adaptation mechanisms! How about that? We haven't discussed international adaptation mechanisms in some time.

"What I'm saying is: If we aren't prepared to go a step further, we're going to sit around here for months to come, looking at each other, going: Well, nothing is fucking happening. What I'm saying is: Nothing will happen until we make it happen. Our visiting politician in all his well-trained rhetoric has put his finger right at the point we have become so good at dancing around in here. Don't you guys understand that?"

The fashionista pushes herself off the wall:

"If we're going there again, I'll be out of here within a minute. I can tell you that."

The sudden move makes her loose dress flow from her bare shoulders even more gracefully than before. The white silk is in a perfect contrast to her dark skin, and once again, I can't help but marvel at the absurdity of her beauty in this particular setting. Her lips are pressed together, tightly.

The ex-banker manages to wrestle his glance away from her and takes a deep breath:

"Stay, please. If you manage, for just a moment, to switch off all the truisms that are swirling around your head about this, and forget all your preconceptions, I think you might even understand me. Look at the out-there, and calmly assess the situation: Look at all the stuff that's going on already, and then look at what's happening as a consequence. Exactly. What's left? That's my question. That's all I'm asking."

I glance around; face for face, we are looking at ourselves. Except for the intruder:

"And what's your answer?"

But the ex-banker doesn't provide one. His words – so cold and cruel – are still in the room. His sentences persist. The dangerous route of thinking he has laid out – not for the first time, but for the first time so clearly, so shamelessly, so strangely convincing – refuses to leave, somehow.

Long, painful minutes pass. No one speaks. No one admits what's happening.

The ex-banker's legs are trembling in a nervous fit. The fashionista is leaning back against the wall. Her large brown bracelets are sinking until both her arms are dangling from either side of her body. Is even she giving in?

Judging from his looks, the brain is taking this route half-way, returning, turning, torn.

It seems that for him, too, the possibilities are coming on, like a slideshow, as we shift our mental control units away from what we have been doing, in here, to what we could do, out there, replacing our theoretical discourse with dare, turning our aspirations into real action. Going one step further – just one step.

Or maybe a few more? The man who is seeing us stretch this for the first time – and stretch it longer and than ever before – is with us, it seems, as our minds slowly smoulder:

How far are we prepared to go? Where, all things considered, is the line, given what's at stake?

Our leader shakes her head.

"Right. If a gelled, shirt-wearing Che Guevara with a car and an MBA has an idea how to move this forward, voila. I'm listening."

Her open palms are pointed at him.

"I don't have one. And neither do you. And neither does anyone in here. Looks like we will have to disappoint our visiting politician? Shame really."

It's not a statement of fact, but a challenge. He doesn't look at her, or anyone, making it.

"Well..."

The leader is taking a deep breath and the ex-banker raises an interested eyebrow and the brain nervously shuffles on his chair, but before she can say anything my man rushes up:

"Shit, I have to go."

I stare at him:

"What?"

He is holding his phone in his hand.

"Looks like someone heard you guys talking."

"What?"

He rushes around and grabs the knob of our door.

"What's happening?"

He turns around.

We're all staring at him, standing there, but he's looking at me – at me! – and there's no answer to our question in his face; there's something else.

Oh, don't look at me like that! Please don't.

"I'll call you."

And with those words, he's gone, and I'm sliding down my chair, and next to me the leader grabs her phone and brings up the feed – is that really what it says? *#blockingparliament?* – and the ex-banker pats my leg:

"Not your boyfriend, eh?"

7

My hill doesn't need special powers. There's no magic involved. Whatever they say, the ditherers and compromisers, everything I need exists: the mills, the panels and the wells. Everything I need – for my network of shared movement; for my give-and-take between flats and offices, north and south, here and there; for a design that unites efficient new insides with beautiful old outsides – is already available. A majestic new grid brings together all the elements of my construct like instruments in a perfectly conducted orchestra.

It started by coincidence, of course. The first time I came up here, I started the drift almost by accident. Inspired by what I had heard in the bare room before, from their, mine, our lips, I simply allowed the flow, dreaming just a little further what we had started to dream... What a moment!

I just sat there on my bench, the way I am now, smiling to myself, as the picture came on. The shapes were still vague, then, no detail to speak of, but I knew instantly that this was the flash I would have to transform; that I would have to try again.

A willingness to walk, just one step further, into our imagination – that's all I need.

There's nothing else to it: I'm crossing the invisible border we are all surrounded by, constantly. I'm leaving, ever so carefully, the realm of the real, the existing, the now, and wander, with wondering eyes, just a tiny bit further, surprised by what I see:

What I always thought was self-evident, isn't; what I always thought was the way it is because that's the way it is, doesn't have to be that way. Not for that reason.

I'm taking one careful step into another kind of future, and as a result whatever my flatmates are hurling at me, bounces off, just like that. As a result, I'm even strong enough to stand up to him:

The technology, my dear visitor, is there. Just take a look around. Just open your eyes.

Yes, there's a spectre haunting the world, the spectre of the blackout, but that's nothing but industry scaremongering. I'm sorry, but you must know that too.

Windmills in people's backyards? My dear visitor. Have we ever asked those living next to a fossil fuel station about their backyards? Have we ever worried how they feel about the dirt in the air, or the ash in their water? I forgot. They tend to be poor and don't have a nice landscape view that could get spoilt a little or the money to give them a voice that's loud enough to make them count.

My dear visitor – if we want to use energy in the future, it seems to me, we will have to make sacrifices.

I imagine how he's staring at me – full of attention.

Because, as much as we like to think so, energy is not a God-given right that comes falling from the sky like rain. It's a precious treasure, a very precious treasure.

And if we're faced with a choice between nineteenth-century ways of producing it, and their emissions, their dirt, their accidents and their detrimental effects on thousands of lives around the world, not to mention the dreadful effect on millions of lives, long term, and what I have started to see – I'm asking you, how hard can it be?

I imagine how he's nodding, full of admiration. I imagine how he's admitting that, yes, you're right, so many solutions have been known for years, and yet: We have ignored them. Knowingly. We have chosen the part of least resistance, because, politically that's the best way to go. Pretty much always. Across parties, across countries. We use any excuse we can. It's that simple. It's that sad.

That's what this very special hill is doing for me. From here, I see how things *could* be, and that's why I know this: There are no more excuses. There's only fear.

8

They're sitting in the middle of the street. Using bicycle locks for chains. Crazy.

Two nervous legs are shaking the words as they come in: *#blockingparliament*.

The hill became my bed when the cold became too much to bear. I'm sitting up, with my blanket up to my knees.

Banner reads: How much louder do we have to scream?

I imagine the others, reading this – the ex-banker in his small studio flat and the fashionista in her house-share of six and the brain at his parents' place. Wherever and whatever home is for our leader, I never learned. Are they as excited?

Police have closed the street further down. A main driveway to parliament is now effectively blocked. Success!

The brain pushes the feed off my screen, and I pick him up on the first ring.

"She says we're only credible if we're joining in, somehow."

"She might be right."

He doesn't respond, as though that wasn't the answer he was hoping I would give.

"What's up?"

"Nothing. I'm looking at the feed."

But there is an unease in his voice. A borderline fear.

"What's wrong?"

"Nothing."

On Friday, we spontaneously walked for a couple of streets, after our visitor had made clear that he'd rather walk alone. It was part of his philosophy, he said, walking: Only when you're putting one foot after the other, do ideas have a chance. Only when you're walking can you be truly free.

During those twenty minutes, I understood something about the brain I hadn't understood before.

What I saw on his face, as he went on about the terrible standstill we're facing, wasn't just frustration, or the temporary loss of hope, or anger. It was sadness; real, heart-wrenching sadness. Seeing him like that, I suddenly understood how desperate the brain is for progress; how much he needs to see this move on; how much he has to *do* something.

Behind the shrewd analysis and the intellectual argument – which I had always thought to be his main stake in the group – there was a heart that seems to be beating for this even stronger than mine: The brain, I felt, beautifully belies his name.

And yet, hearing him on Friday, I also heard something else, and it's in his voice again now:

"I cannot do it."

"What?"

"The blockade. I cannot be part of it."

"We haven't even decided that... We haven't decided anything. What is it? Are you afraid? I am."

"She's organised the chains already, she told me."

"Really?"

Our leader occasionally mentioned her activist friends to us: They've acted more physically than most of us ever would, she said, and we all joined her, I felt, in her admiration for them. Some of them were in the tents, others had been on tracks or runways. She often told us about civil disobedience too – especially in the days around the first coal chain; the one we took part in – and who she had just borrowed on the topic from her local library.

But I kept asking myself: How do we fit in? How do I fit in, as an ordinary woman?

"Let's talk about things first."

"It's... It's my parents. Anyway, you should be there. You should all be there, I think. I'm sure she will call you any minute."

"Your parents?"

"I'll tell you another time. Let's not block the line any longer, okay?"

"Okay."

"I'll be up all night, anyway. There's no way I'll sleep with my screen going crazy like that."

Re-feed in solidarity.

"Okay, I'll be in touch."

"And…"

There's an uncomfortably long pause – he's either reading something, or doesn't know what to say.

"Are you okay?"

"It's happening, isn't it? It really is."

The brain is gone before I can say Yes. A nervous feed returns, but my eyes are drifting elsewhere.

If he was here now your shadow could be drawing on our naked bodies in a tender black. Instead, it's wasted. If he was here now he might be asking if you are my tree and I would smile, happy that he remembered. And I would tell him how you're not blossoming yet, not like most trees around here. Maybe, it's because you're so big? Or you just don't blossom.

It's just a little slower than the others, he would probably say – always a rational explanation at hand.

Just the way he *explained* to me that it's no longer moral to have children, these days: There are too many of us as it is, he said, scrambling over whatever little is left.

Don't you agree that, maybe, that's just a convenient excuse for him not to confront himself with the issue? He didn't respond when I told him that.

He isn't sure about marriage, either, he said, because he sees so very few married couples who manage to keep their love going. Most of them just muddle on, he said, for the sake of it, because they don't have the audacity to divorce. If you stop gambling, you stop living, I told him. At least he smiled.

Isn't it funny how we keep holding up marriage as the ideal – only to keep failing to meet it?

I told him that we wouldn't have most TV drama without it, or the best political scandals, or most popular fiction, but, mainly, I told him that, maybe, he just hasn't met the right person yet, and that's when he kissed me.

If he was here now, lying next to me on this bed, I would ask him what love means to him.

We talked so much that night, in our shared bed, but I would never have dared to ask a question like that.

He would probably have mumbled something about there being no truth in big questions like that. That it's all bound to end in vagueness. Just the way he lectured our group. *Truth is in specifics*. What does he know?

He could have surprised me, of course – you never know with him, I feel. There's so little I know, and yet: I seem to know him so well.

He could have said: This, right here, is what love means to me. What I mean is what is beating inside of you, and what I mean is what is beating inside of me… What I mean is that they are connected, somehow.

I like that, don't you? I like that very much.

But are they? Connected. Whatever is beating inside of him and whatever is beating inside of me.

What do you think?

He.

What do you think?

Me.

Maybe, if he was here now, he would whisper his answer into my ear now, and tickle me with his words. And maybe he would slide down my heated cheek afterwards, and find my lips, and stay, until I'm absolutely certain it's there, the kindling that's the beginning. But he isn't here.

My phone flashes our leader's name. Sometimes, I feel my entire life has been lived like that, neither here nor there. As though one part of me is already gone, while the other is still saying its hushed goodbyes. Sometimes, I feel I've never been a fully committed member of anything at all. As though I'm always about to leave. As though I've always only just arrived. As though I'm always about to leave again.

"Our room. In half an hour. Hurry up. We're going to do this."

9

I know: If I want to move ahead with my hill, I need to gather new hints, bring home fresh evidence. New specifics need to be allowed to enter my picture – without destroying what already exists – so my cautious first draft stops being merely a city and becomes a core. A centre from which everything can flow.

I know that, if I want to make progress, the alternative I've started to see needs to become more robust, almost real enough to enter. Only then will I be able to prove to everyone what I'm already convinced about: We're handcuffed to the way we're doing things because that's the way we're doing things. And for no other reason.

That's what my hill has already taught me beyond all doubt: We might be trapped. But we are only trapped by what we, ourselves, created. The constraints we live under are our own; that's what I'm seeing underlined every time I sit down on my bench now.

We, ourselves, have the keys. When will we have the courage to pick them up?

10

The metal is cold in my fingers as I pass it to the fashionista, but around my ankles, my jeans help.

"Faster!"

My hands are shaking.

"Come on guys."

There was no time for a real decision, and her enthusiasm left no space for concern. Now it's too late. Her end snaps and we're complete.

"Down!"

Our leader jerks me to my knees and we're crouching in a wave: she, then me, then the fashionista. The moment the ex-banker joins us, we're down, collectively.

"Link your arms!"

She presses us together on my right and I do the same with the fashionista on my left. Our leader is the only one who knows what the hell we're doing.

"Don't squeeze me like that."

The fashionista.

"Sorry."

The ex-banker shuffles:

"Better?"

The shaking moves away from my hands, up my arms, and our leader must be feeling it:

"Are you okay?"

I nod, weakly.

The street lamp above us is our only spotlight. Beyond that, there's darkness. The city is still half-asleep.

That's all I see: the grey concrete that stretches beneath us, in all four directions; we're right in the street's middle. And their uniformed legs, unmoved.

They weren't there when we ran into position, but stepped forward the moment we sat down.

There's three of them on either side of the street, I think. I have no idea what's going on in their heads. I have no idea what they're about to do to us.

I raise my head a little.

Further down the street, others have started to wave away the cars that can't pass; the cars that can't pass because of us. Because we're in the way. My arm won't stop.

The air is still wet with night. Or is that my sweat?

There was no time to worry; there was no time to disagree. Looking at each other inside the bare room, our eyes revealed what our hearts knew we had to do. Whatever our heads were trying to say.

"Don't abuse the progress we have made in the last few months to excuse your inaction!"

She shouts the words as though the politicians she means are standing right in front of her.

"Stop running away!"

Her red curls prevent me from seeing her face, but nothing obscures the passion in her voice:

"Stop dithering!"

She presses my shivering arm closer to her body and I instinctively do the same with the fashionista:

"Stop shying away!"

Me?

"Stop shying away!"

And this time, I say it loud enough for everyone to hear. The fashionista turns at me in surprise, but I keep looking ahead and then, so does she:

"Stop... ducking."

Her voice is weak, but not when she repeats her words, squeezing my arm as she does.

"Are you listening?"

The ex-banker's voice, raised like that, sends a shiver down my spine. But it's my own voice that drives me:

"We need you to give us what you're not used to giving us anymore!"

There's no script; none of this has been discussed.

"A decision!"

Her voice croaks as she delivers my punchline. The fashionista has lost all her weakness:

"Yeah. Slap your fists on your table in there and say it out loud and clear. This is the way we're going do it."

"No U-turn when another opinion poll comes around."

I can feel how the blood is leaving my cramped legs, but there's no way to change my position.

"We need you to stick with it."

"And stick up for it."

"We need you to face the flack and see it through."

Everything that's coming out of our mouths is raw and uncontrolled:

"We want action!"

"Now!"

The fashionista turns to me and there's a smile in her voice:

"Unobedience, baby."

Our leader shakes her head, on my other side:

"Disobedience. It's called disobedience."

"Whatever."

I'm smiling in-between them. The leader:

"Action!"

Me:

"Now!"

The fashionista:

"Action!"

He:

"Now!"

Without synchronisation, four mouths are becoming one and that's when it floods me, like sudden dizziness, how every single person could become the central part of this, an irreplaceable element. How everyone could end up making the most essential contribution to this collective demand for change:

"Action!"

"Now!"

It's all within our reach; so close I can almost touch it. But then I hear a voice that's not ours:

"You are obstructing a public driveway. This is an unlawful activity. I must inform you that we are going to remove you."

He has stepped forward, and now the other legs are doing the same, on either side of us.

At the sight of this, our leader's shouts are turning into frantic screams:

"Spineless vote-chasers!"

But only the ex-banker joins her:

"Flip-flopping harlequins!"

In front of me, the concrete is turning police-light blue, but all I see is him, suddenly.

Sitting at a desk to our back, he is probably working on a response to what we're up to, right now, feverishly typing up words of condemnation.

But the picture I'm really seeing is of him in his kitchen, the morning after our shared night, still without a T-shirt, clutching his party's last election slogan, the black mug in a stark contrast to the naked flesh of his chest. I remember his dark blonde hair, shining brightly in the morning sunshine that came falling through the window. Almost golden.

That's when he told me his side of the story. I looked up at him in encouragement.

I was very young then, he said, and everything spoke for it: my interest in old ideologies, my parent's enthusiasm, my feeling that something was rotten with the world and that I wanted to change it somehow. What better place for it than politics, right?

His shoulders are broad, but not too broad. This is where they sagged:

From the first moment on, I did everything I was told to do in order to get where I wanted to get, the degree, the internships, the pleasantries to people I found decidedly unpleasant. I accepted the assistant's job as a natural way in, because it promised, I was assured, lots of ways to step up.

Of course I haven't stepped up anywhere at all in my four years in there, and well, if I look at those above me now, I'm not so sure I want to step up anymore. Anyway.

He had a sip from his coffee, and then another:

It must be so difficult for anyone who isn't inside the political system to understand what it's like. And I can't stress enough how much I don't like what it is like.

On the street, someone has bent down in front of me, clutching my ankles.

I'm trying to remember how our leader instructed me to behave at this point, standing in the semi-darkness of the bare room earlier, but the officer is smiling:

"Don't worry, it won't hurt."

I look at her.

"But I'm afraid it's my duty to remove you."

Someone else reaches through my arms from behind. The same is happening to the others. Neither of us is saying a word.

"Anyway, thank you."

She says this straight to my face.

"Thank you?"

"Yes, thank you."

One of them counts to three and then we're in the air, all four of us, still united by our chains, and the officer smiles:

"I have children too."

11

They carried us to the pavement, and we readily allowed for our chains to be unlocked, as discussed. One officer wrote down our names and addresses, before his colleague wished us a pleasant day. The entire procedure lasted less than half an hour.

We walked away, hand in hand, still unsure what we had done. Still unsure what it all meant.

When I turned my head, at the street's end, I could see that another group had taken our place already.

There is a God, after all, our leader said and her voice trembled with the joy of a young child, kneeling beneath the Christmas tree. For a moment, she had the softness of an angel – and I really loved her like that.

I can still hear those words now, and I'm still feeling the hug she gave me, shortly afterwards – long and warm and genuine. It was the first physical contact between us, I think.

Our kitchen is empty as I enter. I fill a glass with water and drink it down half-way.

From the street, I took the nearest bus to the office as though nothing had happened, booted my computer and started staring at my spreadsheets.

Are spreadsheets to the twenty-first century what the conveyor belt was to the last? Are offices our factories? Are we all but slaves to our screens? Today was the first day since starting this job I didn't ask myself these questions; today, everything passed right past me. My colleagues were nothing but ghosts to me, their words: air.

I drink the rest of my water and re-fill the glass. My breathing is back to normal, but nothing else is.

All day, the rhythm that came to us on that street clocked my pulse, the rhythm that came out of nowhere.

Feeling the others next to me, I felt more than their bodies. Hearing us, I heard more than our voices. Linking arms, we were more than members of a group. Playing my part, I was more than I used to be.

I have another few gulps of water, place the glass on the sink and walk towards my room.

The blockades lasted all day. Whenever the police carried one group away, a follow-up wasn't far behind. It was hard to believe. My favourite arrived this afternoon. *#blockingparliament*, which I had open in one window throughout the day, went wild with it:

There's a mum, a dad, three daughters and a dog. He's the only one not in chains.

It took no more than a few hours for those who had a little more experience with action of this kind to share their expertise, their tips and, in some cases, even their equipment. Seasoned activists and absolute beginners worked hand in hand, while the feed kept pushing our message further and further – into virgin territory.

That's what's best: The vast majority of those on that street today are doing what they are doing for the first time in their lives.

This isn't about professional trouble-making, the trained tactics of a well-known minority, but about people like us. These blockades are the purest, most direct way for us to express how we really feel. Something remarkable has opened up today.

Falling shut, my door seals the darkness. I take a few steps until I'm standing at the edge of my bed.

This evening, the sky was a milky blue more usual in its early morning version. The unruly branch that hangs out onto the pavement from our neighbour's front garden seemed to take the same colour. Passing underneath, I didn't look up.

Is it called leaves when it's a willow? The one I saw earlier had them in a rich yellow, like shiny golden hair, only infinitely more gracious. The trunk rose in sexy hip swing, ready to entice whoever cared to look. And you? Still not a bud.

I'm standing in front of my bed, looking out: Weren't your branches once a glorious homage to randomness?

Now, it seems, they have all started to point into one direction – even now, after everything that has happened. I know – my imagination knows more about him than I do, but I no longer feel where my imagination ends, and I begin.

Out there, it's all just one route now, and at the end there's him, whispering into my ears how much it all means to him. How glad he is to have met me. How much he wants this to become more, so much more. But the sigh I hear comes out of my own mouth.

I pull my jumper over my head in one swift move and don't bother to calm my electrified hair afterwards. The bra I'm wearing is the bra he saw. I felt the cups of his fingers that night, not its thin straps, when they were sliding down my arms, slowly…

There it is, so close – a land where a cut-off isn't a mere formality; where words, however banal they may seem, can mean the world; where pain torments, and joy exhilarates; where what you're giving comes back extrapolated; where all you want to do is give. But I'm not being allowed in. Something is in the way.

I unbutton my trousers and that's when I see myself, alone in my bed, not just tonight, but tomorrow night, and the night after that, and the night after that, and all the nights to come, and something starts to crawl up inside of me as I push my trousers down: Have I gone much further with this than I thought?

I kick away my trousers without looking where they land. Have I gone too far?

Kneeling against the mattress brings you in a better view, your branches unusually nervous, almost jittery: What do you mean, I haven't gone far enough? What about freedom where freedom is due? What about breathing space? What about all the rules in my book?

I push myself off, turn and sit, but getting my tree out of sight doesn't silence its hollow laugh: What do you mean, am I finally getting this? I let myself sink onto my pillow and then it's the sky I see. It's dark grey tonight, just the way I saw it from my hill yesterday.

Hold on – is that it? I pull my naked legs towards me. *The constraints we live under are our own.*

Isn't what's true for the world true for me too? Isn't what's true up there true down here?

My tree's laugh is turning into a careful cheer. All my rules are flowing at me, everything that has prevented me from going one step further, all my *constraints*.

I shake my head, slowly rubbing my pillow. The warning sign is showing itself for what it really is.

Aren't the constraints we impose on ourselves in the name of freedom the most oppressive of them all?

I push myself into a seated position, swinging my feet out of bed, seeking ground. I made these laws – doesn't that mean I can amend them too? Doesn't that mean I can abolish them? There's no judge in this, but me – right?

I imagine my tree, in my back, smiling the smile of a wise man who has just witnessed, full of delight, how a grandchild has understood something very important.

But I don't look at my tree; I grab my phone. *The constraints we live under are our own.*

12

An hour later, he's sitting next to me on my bench, hands pressed between his legs, shoulders slumped forward. He seems tense, and not entirely with me.

Down there, the reds, whites and oranges of all my cities are shining like one. Once again, it feels as though memory itself is glowing in the dark. What I'm seeing isn't so much a city, but a past, ready to be transformed – by me. But not tonight.

"What do I want? So that's why you ordered me here. I assume you mean... with regards to you?"

I turn at him, but he's gazing at the lights.

"You're assuming correctly."

Up here, there's none of the intimacy or warmth that helped to make our previous encounters so special. That's why I insisted on the hill as our meeting point – up here, we have to create everything ourselves.

"It's... difficult."

"I wonder if that answers it?"

"Don't be so quick. I hate when people are so quick and take not having an answer straight away for the answer they don't want to hear. That's just like in politics. You're always expected to have an answer straight away. And if you don't? Well, you better make one up. Which is what everyone is doing all the time, of course. It's the opposite of being honest."

I nod.

My hair still feels wet where my V-neck exposes my shoulders. The sleeved shirt I'm wearing isn't nearly warm enough for the location or the time, but comfort wasn't on my mind when I slipped into it after my hasty shower. The black and white stripes are loose around the three-quarter arms, but not elsewhere.

He's in a dark grey shirt, similar to the one I first saw him in.

"You feel pushed around?"

He turns, finally, and I nod:

"A little maybe."

"It's not my intention to push you around. Believe me."

"Well, what *is* your intention?"

My tone thrills me the way children are thrilled by acts of mischief they know they shouldn't commit – only that I'm absolutely certain I'm doing the right thing.

"I don't know what I want, is my answer to your question."

"Ah yes, any answer would have been better than that one."

"It's such a cliché, I know. But what if it's true? Quite often clichés are true, right? I really don't. I wish it was different. You wouldn't have preferred a lie, would you?"

I turn away and cross my arms in front of my stripes:

"It's your ex, isn't it?"

"No."

"You're still thinking of her, aren't you?"

"Here's what I didn't tell you last time: The love didn't just stop. I ended the relationship. Our world became too small for me. I wanted more. I wanted others."

"Right. I experienced that myself. Your world?"

"That's what it is, isn't it? You create your own world. You define yourself against all others. Making a pair, it's creation. It's art, in a very special kind of way."

"Big words. By your standards, I mean."

"And it can work so well. Until someone crashes into your world, or until one of you wants to break out. You know, is this really the person I want to spend the rest of my life with?"

"And?"

"The thing is: I've started to question the entire concept. Is this really the way we're supposed to do things?"

"A fine addition to that disillusionment pie you're baking, isn't it? How else are we supposed to do things?"

"I just feel all the freedom that's suddenly flowing through my body. During my years in a relationship, I didn't even notice I was missing it. But I did. All the time, I think. All these possibilities I suddenly see. It's something... I can't name it. I can't handle it. I don't really understand."

He hasn't taken out his hands from between his legs:

"I've been thinking: How much love do I need? How much love do I want?"

"Only someone who has too much of it can ask these questions. Or had, until very recently. Everyone else is feeling it too painfully..."

"Feeling what?"

What you've started to fill for me – do you understand?

"Never mind."

"My ex, she found a new one sooner than one-two-three. I saw them the other day. An old friend of ours. I always had some idea. Seeing them together I realised: Maybe we weren't made for each other the way we thought we were. The way we talked about the future, all the time. Our future. It seems so pathetic, looking back."

"Funny thing, isn't it? The future."

"It's the most precious we have, I think. Because we can shape it. Anyway. What is this all about?"

"This hill? It's kind of special. And a little hard to explain. I'll tell you about it later, okay? Maybe."

The pooled human intelligence that's going into what I've started to see – from here – is visible in every appliance, through every window, along every new power line we have constructed. Maybe that's the way I will explain it to him. Or maybe not.

The most precious we have keeps flowing, invisibly, yet for everyone to see, as it's being invested, again and again, in improving what's already better than anything that's been there before.

What I've started to see – from here – makes so much sense, I can't believe there was ever anything, but this.

"So. I saw you were part of... it... this morning."

"How do you know?"

"How was it?"

There's no way to explain this to anyone who hasn't seen our faces, who hasn't heard our shouts, who hasn't felt our chains. We have gone one step further – and what a step.

But what would he understand about the magic we felt on that street?

"It was... important."

"I still can't believe it went on all day. It's... Anyway, that's not why we're here, is it?"

I'm surprised – it used to be the other way round, him steering the conversation where, now, he doesn't want it.

If we keep this going, everything could be possible. It all depends on the coming hours; it all depends on the coming days. This could be the turning-point, a popular explosion, absolutely momentous. This is *it*.

"What did you think about the blockades? I was thinking about you on that street. A lot."

"Have you seen the tree over there?"

"Of course I have seen the tree over there. I'm here almost every night. But what about the blockades? They could change absolutely everything, don't you think?"

"It's very pretty, I think. But probably not as pretty as your tree."

"My tree?"

"The one in your garden. The one you told me about."

He did remember! I lower my head to hide my smile, but I wasn't quick enough, I fear.

"No tree beats my tree, but this one is very beautiful too. The longer you look at it the more beautiful it becomes. I've started to think of looking at these things as preserving them. The longer and harder I look, the more I'm sustaining them. It's as if I'm rescuing them from the flow. Sorry. Maybe I'm going a bit far with this."

"Not at all. I think it's very beautiful."

The way he grabs my eyes floods me with a sense of unity so strong I forget – everything.

I put my hand in his lap. His fingers are warm, despite the night. I feel that my knee is touching his, ever so slightly, but neither of us has broken what our eyes keep holding:

In there, I can arrive – if only you allow me to. With you I can just be – if that's what we both desire.

His hand is stroking me beneath my sleeve now. I can feel a new warmth, spreading from there.

"I need to ask you this one more thing."

The way I've been treating my laws has strengthened me, it seems; honesty is fuelling honesty.

He nods.

"If you're just fine on your own, for which I don't blame you by the way. I mean, I've been like that for years... But then... Then, I don't know: What is this?"

"What do you think it is?"

"No. What do *you* think?"

He comes out of my sleeve. I can feel the cups of his fingers, as they crawl up my stripes, and across my shoulders.

His hands are soft on my neck, his breathing warm against my face. Our noses are close enough to touch now, his soft lips where I wanted them all week.

The silence he keeps stretching only intensifies the sparkling green I'm such a willing hostage to.

"The most wonderful thing that has happened to me in years."

I can't even stare at him in response.

I can't even swallow.

Before I know it, I'm returning what I'm receiving, multiplied by a longing that has been frustrated a few nights too many.

How I missed your taste! How I missed what your tongue is doing to my inside!

I raise my hands to his shoulders, and for a long moment, our lips don't allow us to reach for words. When we part, there's that smile again. I'm smiling too:

"Please tell me that you won't run away again when we reach the bottom of the hill, okay?"

"I might get kidnapped."

"Well, I guess, that can be arranged. But I have to warn you. The way I kidnap people – it might involve some slow torture."

He raises an eyebrow.

"Of a sexual nature."

I slide my hand into his hair. It's soft around my fingers. They tenderly scratch his head.

"Just don't expect me to resist too much."

All the places my imagination has taken me in the last few days are merging on your face, and I'm kissing it.

Your nose, your cheeks, your chin – I'm kissing everything I see. Shifting up my leg, I'm sliding over yours until I can pull you close, hook-style. Your hand comes around my waist, tightly. You touch me where my journeys never got. Do you know that?

Our lips, when they find each other again, block everything that doesn't belong here, in our world, and I'm no longer able to consider consequences, weigh my options, think, but you keep pressing whatever is beating inside of me against whatever is beating inside of you, and whatever is beating inside of me is closer than it's ever been to not just beat – but burn.

Can you feel it? Do you know what I'm about to do?

Three

Because We Can

I let go – and that was the end of it, as much as I would love to pretend otherwise.

"I can't fucking believe this."

They are my thoughts exactly, of course, but it's not me, shouting them out loud. It's the brain.

And he's shouting them for a different reason:

"I can't believe this."

He's sitting in the bare room's centre, alone, staring at the handcuffs that are being displayed on his phone.

His forehead is not just in wrinkles, but in agony. If he had more hair, it would be standing in all directions today, I think. The crumply dark blue he's wearing atop his jeans has unbuttoned sleeves, but they haven't been rolled up properly.

The brain is showing me a side of him he doesn't usually allow to come through.

But I'm still in my head. *I like being kidnapped by you.* I'm still in my bed. Three days ago.

There was the greedy kissing, the desire to feel and be felt. There were the silent moans that should have been screams if only my flatmates hadn't been at home. There was the wanting each other, the raw, honest, unashamed wanting of another body – but behind it all there was more.

Behind it all, there was the magic that turns sex into more than sex, the unexplainable chemistry than turns a physical act into an overpowering swell. We let ourselves go in our giving, certain that what was going on was the uniting of two beings that simply had to unite, a mutual penetration: inevitable.

Sinking into him that night, I felt like I had never made love before, and the realisation still sends a shiver down my spine, even now.

"I mean, look at this. I can't stand it any longer."

He's holding up his phone to me. I'm slouched on a chair next to him, nodding:

"I know. I've seen the pictures."

He looks at me:

"Yes, you look like you haven't slept much, either. If you don't mind me saying so."

I just nod.

I'm not sure whether he's referring to the brown mess on my head, which I didn't manage to get washed before I rushed to work this morning, or my eyes, which are tired to the point I don't even notice anymore.

My arms are hanging down on either side of my birch-coloured work blouse.

Here's what I should have felt too, that night: Withdrawing from me in my bed, it wasn't just his penis, wrinkling into the defensive. The strange speechlessness that followed our shared orgasm wasn't just his physical exhaustion.

The fact that he didn't turn around – not just once – when he walked away from my front door in the morning was more than a slip, the silence since: no accident.

He confirmed it all half an hour ago. With a single message. With one cruel word.

My phone has handed him five forthright messages since he left me that morning, three days ago, each of which took me half an hour to compose.

I wonder how long it took him:

"Sorry."

I sleepwalked into the trap, and the trap snapped hard. I push myself up:

"We could have known this, I think."

I cross my arms in front of my chest. The brain looks up from his phone:

"The clearing?"

"*I* could have known this. Yes, the clearing. And the legal monstrosity that's making it possible."

He adjusts his glasses:

"Of course we could. But..."

There it is again – it's in his eyes, I think.

"But?"

I look at him in expectation, but before he can say anything the fashionista storms in:

"Man, this is killing me."

She kisses me first, then him, and slumps onto a chair, stretching a low waist yellow from beneath a loose jumper in red. The brain shakes his head:

"What did you expect, invitations to their Christmas party?"

"Shut up."

It's as though, within a moment of her arrival, the brain is back to normal.

The fashionista crosses her arms:

"I don't know what I was expecting, but not... this."

"It was only a matter of time."

"Fuck that."

It's as though the side he's just shown to me – the passion, the frustration, the tension – is gone, completely. As though he's only showing it to me.

I can't help thinking that it's due to the walks we shared this week. They satisfied a mutual need, I think. Walking and talking, we got to know each other better – and I'm worried.

"To be honest I'm surprised this cat-and-mouse has been going on for that long. I mean, it's been three days."

"And what three days, too!"

"Yes, but the blockades have turned into an international embarrassment for this government. I mean, weekend demonstrations – who cares? Shows the healthy state of a democracy, after all. Disruptions at a power station are for the power company to deal with. And, obviously, they're not too bothered either. But this? This is a very public display of their failure."

"What bugs me most is the way it's been done, you know, no press conference, no announcement. I mean, what did they think? That we wouldn't notice?"

"Look, it's only a minor amendment."

I wonder if the mock-politician voice I've just used is really a mock-him voice. The fashionista laughs:

"My arse yes."

"Rest assured, lawyers around the world have started to feed the truth. We keep trending, if for all the wrong reasons."

The brain points at his phone.

"What are they saying?"

"It's the most drastic emergency measure in years. Decades even."

"You have to understand. It's all about national security. It's all in your interest."

Mocking him in this room seems more therapeutic than anything I've tried so far – random chats on the network, long walks, the hill (in vain), ridiculous conversations with my tree, two and a half bottles of red wine.

"You know, I was thinking earlier. In a hundred years or so, students will look back at us and wonder: What the hell was that mysterious concept they used to excuse the kind of behaviour we're usually learning about when we're learning about dictatorships? Don't you think?"

She looks up to the brain the way you would to a teacher, wanting appreciation for her thoughts.

"Because, by then everything will be so obviously inter-thingy –"

"Twined."

"Yes. They'll be laughing their heads off. National security? You got to be kidding, right?"

She's clearly disappointed by his meek smile. Not even the bait of an intellectual discussion seems to get him today; nothing is able to penetrate his strange mood:

"Yes, but right now, those two nouns are still enough for a government to do pretty much whatever it wants to do. As on display out there."

She's nodding and I'm nodding too, even though I'm not really here. It's not just my hill that has stopped working, it seems; so has the bare room.

"Did you see the police officer counting earlier?"

"Counting?"

The brain looks at her.

"Some bystander filmed it. The officer says to this guy, the mechanic: You're going to prison for that. The guy says, very calmly, why he's there, you know, that he's no no longer able to be part of what he considers a terrible wrong without inflicting wounds on his conscience, and that he's withdrawing support for the government for that reason and that this is his way of showing it, but the police officer starts counting instead."

"What do you mean counting?"

"Months in prison. It was such a scene. One, two, three. That speed. As if he was the judge."

"Street justice. That's where we're at right now."

He shakes his head.

Forget what I said about God, our leader texted a few minutes ago. She sounded unusually downbeat: We're all alone. Each and everyone of us. Stumbling on.

"It's all hard-core enforcers out there now. That's the problem. All the nice guys are gone. Replaced by these machines. Believers in change must not apply."

"The problem is: His numbers are probably right."

"Fuck, really?"

She stares at him.

"Yes. For people like you and me, people like us, people like the ones that were out there on that street, people with jobs and families – that's the end of it. They're putting us back where we belong. They're shutting us up. Very effectively too."

There it is again:

"We might have lost more than we've gained with this."

It's in his eyes.

He lowers his head. His phone has just announced a text. The fashionista gets up:

"Shit, I'm going. This room has turned into a fucking depression zone. Honestly."

She starts for the door:

"What's the point sitting around here like that?"

When I move from her to the brain, he hastily turns away his phone from me:

"I'm off too, actually. Time for me to reacquaint myself with my criminally neglected desk at work. There's lots to catch up on, I suppose."

"Right."

He stands up and I look back at the fashionista, who, doorknob in hand, is shaking her head:

"Where's the rest of our lousy gang anyway? Looks like the others have given up already."

Picking up his jacket from behind him, the brain doesn't look at either of us as he speaks, but she's not bothering to wait for an answer, anyway, and I'm still elsewhere, really:

"I don't think they are missing because they have given up."

2

I still don't understand how something that looked so promising could swing into its ugly opposite, so quickly.

For a moment, it really looked as though this was it: an activity associated with far-away countries, for far-off causes, in times long gone and not to return – on our streets!

For a moment, it really looked as though the majority of the population was applauding the bravery of those that were holding their elected leaders to account a little more physically, because, for a change, they weren't seeing others, out there, but themselves. On that very street. In those very chains.

But the government has managed to spin our coming-together into an expensive disruption of what really matters – as though it was them standing in classrooms, breaking up fights, cleaning up the vomit in hospital rooms. As though they couldn't just walk into the parliament building, instead of taking their cars.

Just as ordinary people started to use their right to stand up, the police is being told to push them down. Gone, by law, is the understanding. Gone, by law, is the sympathy.

As for the media – they have fallen back into their old ways the moment the heavy-handed crack-down gave them a chance to, obsessing about the alleged extremism of our actions, when nothing could be further from the truth. Now, colourful slideshows have given way to what they think is the defining image of the week, our coming-together in handcuffs.

The government has robbed us of our last option; they ignored the furthest we can go.

Now, any way forward is cocooned in a crust that looks so thick and clotted, I think it's indestructible.

What could our wedge possibly be? How are we meant to break this? What's still left? I just don't see it.

3

"I have no idea what he's trying to tell me. I mean, what the fuck, a real signal?"

The fashionista lowers the ex-banker's text message. I checked into the bare room out of desperation; why she's here I'm not sure. We're both sitting on the table in the middle, hands underneath our legs, legs dangling. *A real signal?*

Terror crawls down my spine as I understand that the ex-banker might have shifted his mental control unit much further than I thought he had. Beyond the blockades... Beyond whatever else?

I shake my head, very slowly:

"I have no idea."

Are the others listening to him? How vulnerable are they to this?

"Anyway, back to your man. Much more interesting, don't you think?"

I turn to her. She's wearing one of those outfits that would look silly on anyone but her: puffed-up trousers in a dark blue, a rose-coloured blouse and a vest I can't even begin describing.

She's negotiating the pretty and the sexy in a way that wows both men and women in the nicest possible way, and I wonder how she manages to hit this delicate position so confidently just about every time I see her.

My work wear makes me look like a character from a black and white film in comparison. I feel painfully dull.

It's Wednesday evening – one week has passed since we shared our bed.

"He's gone. Haven't you been listening? Gone, gone, gone."

"What's his problem then?"

"If only I knew."

If only he knew.

"Let me guess: He thinks he can have all these other girls, is that it? The Casanova syndrome."

All weekend, I have been imagining him eyeing up others in a lightness reserved for those who, momentarily, don't ask for anything. All weekend, I've seen how content he must be right now, enjoying the excitement of the self, unrestrained.

"It might even be true, that's the problem. From what I've seen, anyway. God only knows what nastiness lurks behind the facade he's kept up with me."

"Fucks with their minds, that."

"What do you mean?"

"The illusion that they can have all these other girls. Gives them one hell of a high, because they don't understand what it actually takes for two people to like each other, let alone love each other."

"I thought he understood that quite well."

Shut up, girl – she's right!

I was a fleeting moment on another male consciousness, one of a hundred tiny dots. Taken together, they might make a picture for him. Individually, they are nothing. I am nothing; I was nothing to the first man in years I actively wanted, rather than to merely just tolerate him.

"You give them a great experience and they twist themselves into believing that it could be the same with all others out there. What they don't get is that to *have us* just means we're taking an initial interest. Everything only happens after that. Fools, really."

Fools indeed.

"I've had my fair share of runaways and ditherers, believe me, honey. It's a modern disease. Or maybe not even a modern one. And I'm not saying it's just men either. We just don't quite know what role we're supposed to be playing anymore. In a different way, I've been just the same..."

"Well, look at you. You really can have them all."

"Same illusion, honey. That's just looks. That's nothing but the outside, which says nothing – nothing at all – about what might go on between two people. It's just that we've become so obsessed by the outside, we don't know what it takes anymore... Anyway, I don't want to bore you with my take on modern love. I've been thinking a bit too much about this, recently, I think."

"Now you're silly. It's good to talk. It's a cold world out there, you know."

"I thought it was warming."

"Oh, shut up."

"Anyway, what the hell's going on with us? It's over isn't it? I mean, no one's coming anymore."

"Yes, it's... I don't know."

"And what's wrong with our brainy friend? He was very strange the other day."

"Yes, I noticed too."

"Why didn't he take part in the blockades, anyway?"

I'm not sure how much I should say. How much of what he told me was just for me.

"You know, he was the first of his family to go to university? The only one to make it in the so-called professional world. His success means the world to his mother and to his father, they've invested all they have in him, financially, and otherwise. Ever since they emigrated here, it was all about him. He doesn't want to let them down. He can't frustrate these expectations."

And yet, the tension that torments him as a result keeps him awake at night, he told me, because if he stays inactive, he might explode. It's that tension I've started to see on his face, but I don't tell her. She takes her hands from underneath her legs:

"At least he's got parents that care. I wish I could say the same about mine."

"Are they –"

"Divorced and not that interested in their daughter anymore, yes. My dad was even considering moving back to our poverty-stricken home country a while ago. Well, his home country. I have no idea what's riding him, but never mind. At least I had a happy childhood. Unlike our red-haired fury in here."

"What's her story?"

"Hasn't she told you? I'm surprised. She broke our rule over that one for me, and for the others too, I think: She lost her dad when she was very young. Her mum brought her up alone, with almost no money. Real hard times. She had trouble at school because of it, and for a long time afterwards. She says it's all down to her growing up without a dad. I'm surprised she hasn't told you."

"Well, we never really talked, you know, personally. I mean, we never have, either."

"You should catch her some day. She can be quite different, outside the bare room, I mean."

"Really?"

She nods:

"Died in a coal mine or something, I think."

"Who?"

"Her dad. How about your family?"

"My family?"

4

I can't talk about my family like a normal person anymore, just the way I can't talk about friends like a normal person anymore. All there is – here, at my junction – are names on the network, dots at the periphery of my consciousness. Ready to fall off any minute. I'm losing my old friends just the way I lost my mum, and my dad, and my sister, and I'm trying really hard not to think about it, but sometimes I lose my strength.

It's my fault; that's the problem. It was my decision to leave – the country I was born in, the house I grew up in, the society that paid for my secondary education. My dreams were too big for the small town I called home, then, and I was bent to correct this error on circumstance: I made the cut. It was *my* choice.

And now, it's as though between that life and what I am now, a curtain has been raised. Sometimes I get to have a peek – at my curly-haired mum in her dark woollen jumper, hugging me with an affection I took for granted, then, before she left the house for her office, or the teacher look my dad used to give me when we talked about my professional future, one hand in the pocket of his jeans, one hand in his neat grey beard.

But mainly I see shadows. Lives I can no longer touch. It's as though there's no connection anymore – between them and me, between then and now.

It's as though everything I did in the last ten years has served this one purpose above all others: to make the curtain stiffer.

5

"That explains a lot, honey."

"Does it?"

"The fact that you've been around that much, yes. Explains why you're... much more mature than the others."

"Am I?"

"In a very good way, yes."

It was the fashionista's idea to drink; it's my fault we're drunk. And the rum's.

We're surrounded by loosened ties and too much make-up. The only reason for this shitty bar was it's vicinity to the bare room. The non-specific dance they're playing must offend her often pronounced R&B sensibilities as much as it quarrels with my vague preference for what they used to call alternative rock.

"You're someone to look up to. For me anyway. Which doesn't happen all that often anymore, you know what I mean?"

I fucked myself up, honey, because I have been around that much, but I'm not going to tell you that. The certainty that followed me through the last ten years has given way to teething, hurtful doubts, but what's that to anyone but me?

I smile at her, innocently. The foundation that used to hold my lifestyle is crumbling, and it's shedding things I don't want to see, but three glasses of rum aren't enough to break my resolve to keep looking away.

"What did you think of me at first? Honest answer."

"Another trendy young girl with funny clothes and too much energy."

"I thought so."

"But that's just, you know, I'm glad we're…"

"Getting drunk together? About fucking time, honey."

Moving her glass away from her lips – which are only very lightly coloured today – something changes on her face:

"It's not going to happen, though, is it?"

"What?"

"The… everything… what did we call it? The Great Turnaround."

I stare at her:

"What do you mean?"

"It's never going to happen. Come on, the group is dead. Let's be honest with ourselves."

"But…"

"It's over, whatever. We'll find something else to do."

"Are you serious?"

I'm feeling shaky, all of a sudden.

"Come on, honey. Look out. We're months away from the most important deadline people have been talking about for years and we're a world away from reaching it. It's obvious, isn't it? In December, the suits will lock themselves in a room again and set another deadline, pacifying everyone, and everything will just go on the way it is. I can't believe we twisted ourselves into believing anything else."

I grab the counter for hold:

"So, you think..."

"The whole process is a charade! A carnival. It's all just one expensive, carbon-spouting parade of finger pointing. Nothing's going to happen. And you don't believe that we're going to stop the drilling if we aren't forced to, do you?"

She shakes her head:

"No way, honey. The failure of the blockades made me see clear again. We're just going to go on blaming each other, because – how convenient! – we have divided this planet into small patches surrounded by artificial borders, which is all we need to forget that it's still one fucking atmosphere, one fucking planet, one fucking future. We'll finger-point ourselves into our graves, honey. Shall we have one more round? Come on. I'll pay."

I nod, slowly, staring into the big black nothing that has opened up in front of me:

"So, you think we're... just going to go on?"

"As we are, yes. And you know why? Because we can. It's that simple. And I can't believe we thought differently in that dark, damp room of ours."

She raises her glass:

"Here's to us, chasers of a fairytale."

I stare at her.

"Here's to us, the vanguard of stupidity! A sad and lonely troupe of idiots."

The carelessness in her face relives mine of all its colour. My disconnected mouth moves in slow motion, but no words are coming out.

6

For me, it's all about the anticipation.

He's lying next to me, saying this in the kind of voice we reserve for when we're lying in bed with someone. Naked. It's our last night. The bed is my bed.

What I mean is: It's not spring yet, but everywhere you look you can see it's about to arrive. I think that's even more beautiful than spring itself. Everywhere you look there's –

This promise?

Exactly. Everywhere, there's this inkling. Even the birds are singing differently, but it's what they're singing towards. It's what they're looking forward to.

It's their praise of things to come?

It's such a powerful moment. The potential is all around us – in the air, in the sun, in every tree.

Amazing, isn't it? The idea that something so small, almost not visible, a tiny bud, the mere hint of a blossom, can become something else...

And then, there's those first few days, when no one can quite believe that it's really happening. When everyone's asking: Do we really deserve this? I don't like those days. Sometimes, that's when I lose interest.

Really?

Yes, he said. Maybe I enjoy the inkling more than the real thing. But, by then, I was already lying on a meadow, somewhere, inhaling the sweet scent of the blossoms, the two of us covered in a warm light, and all I wanted was to stay like that forever, resting my head against the shoulder of a man who had talked to me about my favourite season in a way no one ever had.

And there was a sense of lightness in the air, a sense that only confirmed me in my letting go, and when I came back, my tree was drawing on our naked bodies just the way I had dreamt it would, on my body... and on yours. *Sometimes, that's when I lose interest.*

7

The only pen I have has fallen to the floor, but bending down will make me vomit.

The fluorescence in the magazine's conference room is bright any day of the week; today, it's brutal. They are sitting around the large table in front of me: three women and four men, plus the editor, who's being looked at by everyone. Me and a few other lower ranks are sitting in the second row, watching.

They are talking the way they do in here: Something is needed on the tar sands. A feature documenting the recent expansion. Another piece on the Arctic, too. I stare at my pen, silent on the grey carpet – I need you.

How the controversy has died down. How another batch of permits has just gone out. How it's all about where things will move once this area has been exhausted.

"You got all that?"

In my skull, yesterday's rum feels like a lake out of which bits of our conversation shoot up like jumping fish.

But the lake's surface still only reflects the face of a man that doesn't want to leave, however hard I try. He's probably sitting at his desk right now, writing up a detailed report on a different kind of opposition, the enemy we used to call our We. How could he have dared to crush us for his own benefit?

Only to leave it at that. Not to be repaired. That's when the split started. With him. The failure of the blockades – that was merely the last hit.

"You got all that?"

But what he did to us doesn't bother me nearly as much as what he did to me and I should have taken my instinct seriously, back on our first table-for-two, when it pointed me right here: at the inevitable end result.

But with every detail he revealed about himself, I liked him more. With every puzzle piece he handed me, the picture I saw got brighter. More beautiful.

I kept pretending – why? Because I was weak enough to believe, then, what I'm still believing now.

"Hello?"

Shit – the editor means me!

"Yes. Yes... Sorry. I got all that."

I smile at him, as confidently as possible, but he's already talking to the table again.

If I don't write down a few words at least I will have forgotten that we talked about the tar sands and the Arctic by the time I'm being let out of this torture chamber.

I bend forward, carefully testing the ground. They're talking about consolidation in the utility sector now. How the recently emerged multinationals can't be stopped on their buying spree. How the competition authorities are keeping quiet about it.

It's either one swift move, or a very slow one – I'm not sure which strategy is less risky. The pen remains silent.

"Got that?"

"Yes."

When is he going to wonder how I'm taking notes without a pen? Tar sands, Arctic, utility consolidation.

I move my hand forwards on my black trousers, still undecided which tactic to employ, and focus on the pen. They're talking about a study now, some kind of survey.

My stomach roars in sickness. I pull back my hand to cover it, but that neither stops the pain, nor does it decrease its embarrassing volume. How, viewed globally, people are, by and large, still of the opinion that things will not have to change drastically when it comes to energy. How that's good news.

It's now or never: I move my hand along my leg, cross the threshold of the knee, concentrate on my stomach, lose all sense of what's happening at the table, bend, swiftly, stretching my fingers, swallow, crouch and grab:

"I'll get it for you."

A hand is holding it up to me. My stomach is louder than my Thank You. I erect myself again, pressing my lips together. A feeling of acute sickness traverses my body like an electric shock in slow-motion. Everything flickers.

When I look up from my empty sheet of paper – tar sands, Arctic and what else? – my unexpected saviour has turned around again, but now the editor is looking at me from the table's end:

"Is our editorial assistant not feeling very well today?"

I hate the patronising voice that comes with his white shirts and his extravagant cufflinks.

"I'm... I'm fine. I'm sorry. I'm feeling a bit hot in here, that's all."

I'm a mess. The time I spent inside the office toilet was more productive than the time I spent at my desk so far.

"We'll be finished soon. Then you can have some fresh air. Go for a walk perhaps?"

He chuckles.

"As long as you're not chaining yourself in the middle of our driveway out there."

I stare at him.

"What... I..."

They are all looking at me now. Everyone has turned; my cheeks are about to explode. It never occurred to me that anyone at work might know about me and the blockades, but they are looking as though they all do. Every single one of them.

"A rather pointless exercise, don't you agree? At the taxpayer's expense, mind you."

He's grinning at me in disdain and, looking around, it's a disdain I can see on all their faces, and all I want, in that moment, is to die, but instead I see what's left of our group, our leader, the ex-banker and the brain, and they feel more distant from me than they ever have, all three of them looking in one direction – the direction the ex-banker is pointing them to. *A real signal.*

Covered in shame, I'm connecting the dots too effectively for anyone's good: The text the brain got and didn't want to be seen in the bare room – from the ex-banker, probably, or from the leader. The ex-banker's suggestive message to the fashionista. And the leader's uncharacteristic silence. If she is quiet the way she is – that can only mean one thing: She is onto something she doesn't want us to know about. Or me, in any case.

Sinking into my own embarrassment, the picture is moving from the back of my mind to its front, and it shows all three of them, very clearly. They're standing arm in arm, looking madly defiant. Looking far too determined.

Can they be serious about this? I wish I could say No.

"Well, thank God that's all over and being dealt with. And we've got a magazine to run, right?"

The editor turns back to the table.

"So, tar sands or Arctic on the cover, what do people think?"

8

She was right: We will never have the audacity to say No before we have to.

We will suck until there's nothing left to suck. We will dig faster, scrape harder, drill deeper – and then we will blow the ground beneath our feet to pieces to claim what the earth is trying to keep with all its might.

He was right, talking to me about this in his kitchen: This is our lifeblood; this is who we are.

And that means we will keep up the burning – until there's nothing left to burn. We will bury the consequences deep down our backyards, and we will dump the waste wherever we won't see it; we will simply carry on.

I'm sitting on my bench, looking down my hill – but nothing is happening.

Everything is just the way it is, just the way we know it. I press my hands between my thighs.

My flatmates were right, too, when they told me I was snobbish about this: We will keep buying more cars every year because they embody everything we stand for and no one – no one! – has the right to deny that to anyone, anywhere. We will fly until the planes start dropping from the sky.

Everyone was right: Humanity will not think and change and turn and whoever says otherwise is either a good liar or a goddamn fool, and I've been both.

Drinking with her has brought out an undercurrent that must have been bursting to show its ugly tongue for such a long time. Reality, the strongest liquor there is.

Our vision was a fancy, our dream a delusion! Our version of a future? A foolish fantasy!

My belief that the impossible is possible – that we can really pull this off – has exploded into a thousand tiny pieces. Hazy remnants of a once mighty idea. Fragments I can no longer touch. All the magic has gone phut.

I'm falling down the wrong side of the wall and, this time round, there's no one here to catch me.

I press my legs together even tighter. I'm lost in hope's murderous shadow, staring at the wreckage of my raised expectations, and there's nothing I can do.

She was right: We will keep going exactly the way we are going right now. *And you know why? Because we can.*

9

That night, I'm lying in bed with my laptop, holding on to what's left, now that the bare room is just a room again, the hill just a hill. Click.

I know it's going to happen; the network won't prevent the attack – click, click.

Timelined and tagged, I'm grinning into the camera from a worn-out mattress I had lying on a rooftop one summer, click, and then I'm sitting on a chair we made out of supermarket boxes once. Click, click.

Everything I've managed to hold back in the last few weeks is about to crash down on me – I can feel it.

Click. I'm drinking from one of those soggy paper cups they gave you in the grubby little café that was just below my flat at the time, click, and then I'm watching a beautiful dawn from the balcony of the attic room that came a few weeks later. Click – who is really steering the network?

Looking at it hurts, but not more than not looking: Thinking of them only brings on the picture I don't want to see. The three of them in a row of radical determination. Ready to push this forward in their own twisted way. I shiver.

And thinking of you only reminds me: You beautifully filled what I wanted to be filled, but in doing so, you also widened it. Do you understand that? I know you're no longer listening.

You're gone, and what is left is bigger and blacker than it has ever been.

Before you, an attack would hurt; now, I feel, that word isn't strong enough anymore.

Click, click – it's all there, how my body used to adapt, slowly, to every one of my eight cities. How my brain expanded or contracted. How my skin changed its colour, my hair its texture. The place I left behind wouldn't let go for days, and sometimes weeks. Random impressions would come flashing in – café tables I had sat at reading, or my favourite park benches, side streets I had walked to clear my mind, or backyards with my neighbours' arguments waving over, or that night's dinner meal. The contrasts always registered; the comparing was constant.

But that's all gone. The slow-burning sensation of yet another transition, click, and the excitement that comes, inevitably, with being exposed to unfamiliar surroundings, click, and the mild shock that was such an important part of the attraction at the time, click, click, click. All gone. Just be, click. Just. Click. Be.

But there's no one to be with and everything I've become so good at holding back in the last few weeks, is flooding in: How do other people live their lives? I really don't know anymore. Click, click.

And it's all my fault; whatever anyone says. What seemed to be without an alternative at the time – now, from my junction, it appears to be the worst option on a long list of alternatives that's continuously running through my head like an electronic share price index.

I thought I'd done exactly what was asked of me, when I turned myself into a voluntarily migrant, the twenty-first century impersonated.

And now? Look at me!

This is what I lied about on our very first table-for-two, the shadow I chose to ignore. All the fragments I managed to keep at bay in the last few weeks are finding each other, and the result is screaming a single sentence at me, over and over again: Everything was a mistake. Everything.

I slam the display shut and my laptop's I'm-asleep-when-you-are-not starts to pulsate through the darkness of my room, radiating my defeat in front of what's deep inside of me, so raw and black and mean – a blurry strip across my empty vision, a pathetic ribbon for what's to come. I'm starting to feel it now, and then I'm feeling that all my protection is gone.

I pull the blanket over my face. Over my peeled result. Over this attack. Over everything.

10

"Jesus, what's the matter with you?"

"Nothing... I –"

"You've been crying."

"No I haven't."

I'm slithering onto the empty chair in front of me. I'm trying not to look up. I didn't expect either of them in the kitchen at this time of night.

"Yes, you have. What's up?"

"Nothing."

"Nothing? Come on, we're not blind."

My outspoken flatmate is slumped onto a chair in the middle of the kitchen.

She is drunk, or in any case, unusually relaxed. Her linen-clad legs are loosely apart, her feet freed from their heels. She has unbuttoned her black blouse the way you only do in the safety of your own kitchen. Whatever has eased her, it's taken away a great deal of her professional tightness, leaving merely her natural exuberance, and I can't help feeling that I like her better that way.

"I just can't sleep, that's all."

"How are the meetings going?"

I stare at my quiet flatmate. She's in light blue pyjamas, hugging a cup of tea that's steaming up her face.

"Oh, you know, fine."

"Just fine? What happened to your enthusiasm?"

"Let's not talk about it."

"Yeah, that's right. You're better off leaving the greening-this greening-that to the eco-hippies, anyway. I mean, come on. That's not really you, is it?"

My quiet flatmate nods at her assessment.

I look up.

Maybe it's the teary, drained state I'm in, or maybe it's the fact that at least one of them is drunk, or maybe there are other reasons for things like this to happen, but I take a deep breath – despite myself. A very deep breath:

"It's not about greening this, greening that. That's the whole point. I wish the marketing and environmental departments of the world had never started to talk about the issue like that."

They're both looking surprised. But they're not the only ones.

"What *is* the point?"

"It's... God, I don't know myself anymore. It's about how we treat this... our shared home, so that it will remain our home, and doesn't turn into a... damn it, into some kind of... burning battlefield."

"Our home? What, this flat?"

"No, not this flat."

I roll my eyes:

"Or, well, actually, let's say yes, this flat. Let's say this flat *was* our planet."

"What?"

"And I'd be like... I'd grab your tea and spill it all over the table, and I'd throw your sugar through the room, and I'd take those bottles and smash them, right here, and I'd ram that pot into the cabinet with all our glasses, and I'd take the bleach from down below and spread it all over the mess I've created."

"What?"

The tears I denied have done something to my voice; there's an unusual vulnerability to it, a fragility that exposes how much I feel what I'm saying:

"And then I'd go: Too bad. Sorry. I'll clean it up some time in the future maybe."

And it makes them listen.

"Very funny. We would make sure you clean it up straight away, darling."

"But instead, I'd set the entire mess on fire."

"Excuse me?"

"I don't know: You wouldn't put up with behaviour like that, would you?"

"Of course not."

"Exactly. None of us would tolerate in our own homes what we're tolerating in our shared home – the one that's all around our homes, whether we like it or not. You know, you can work as hard as you can to create your perfect place in this world, but it's still going to be on this planet. It's still going to be beneath our one atmosphere. We all share it – and we're all responsible for it."

"Right."

"Right."

"I know how far this used to be for me. How nicely out of sight: Nothing to do with me. Nothing at all. But if I've realised one thing in the last few months than it's that the so-called environment – that's us. Us, right here."

"Us too?"

I'm nodding.

"But we keep wrecking it to the best of our abilities. Day by day, we're ramming pots into cabinets full of our best, most precious glasses and we see them splinter right in front of our eyes and we don't think the first thing about it."

Something is going on – I can see it on both of their faces. Neither of them seems to know what to say. Instead, they get up, almost simultaneously:

"I'm going to bed, I'm really tired now. Anyway… thanks. See you tomorrow."

"Yes, thanks."

I hear how one door closes and I hear how another door closes and then, there's silence again.

I shake my head. Given what happened to me before I entered this kitchen, I should ignore what has just happened inside of it for the sake of my own safety.

I should look the other way immediately, I know, but, somehow, I can't.

For the sake of my own sanity, I should run as fast as I can, but, somehow, I'm not being allowed to get away. Somehow, I'm unable to narrow my point of view the way I'd sworn I would, earlier – back to normal, back to where everyone else is – and settle in a position of comfort. Something inside of me, it seems, has been a little too hot recently to fade without a fight.

I can almost see myself elsewhere too. I can almost see myself, sticking my head through the curtain, even – very, very carefully. Speaking to *them*?

I can't help the smile that's carefully testing the ground. Thinking of everything I have seen, felt and done in the last few month, is this really what I have come to? Halted, halfway. Stuck in-between, once again. Neither here nor there. Am I really prepared to accept that?

I get up.

Thinking of everything I have seen, felt and done in the last few weeks: Am I really prepared to let him go like that?

11

"I want you to call him. Here. Phone. Dial. Speak. You know how it works?"

The fashionista is pointing at my phone that's lying on the table between us.

It's the following day – Friday – and we're sitting inside the bare room. It seemed the easiest place to meet. I managed to leave the office shortly after five. The air in here smells unused, almost mouldy.

"What do you mean?"

I'm hiding my work wear beneath a buttoned-up jeans jacket; she's not hiding a red jumper that exclaims in bold letters that she's not to be messed with. She answers by grabbing my phone:

"Here, let's see, last calls – not calling many people, these days, are you? Date? Is that what you saved him as, date?"

"Well, he hasn't given himself much of a chance to become more than that, has he?"

"I'm not so sure, from what I heard. Anyway – here, it's ringing. Give him some shit, honey!"

She's holding the phone against my ear.

"You're crazy... I'm not..."

"Not crazy at all."

"What about freedom and –"

"Fuck off, freedom. We're all on our knees in front of that altar all the time, not being pushy and shit. If you want to be independent you shouldn't be on your knees, right?"

"But..."

I'm holding the phone myself now: ring, ring.

"Real independence is only possible if there's some commitment too, and honesty."

Ring, ring.

"It's just that..."

"He'll calm down, believe me. It might take some time, or it might happen very sudden – when he realises what's at stake. Where the hell is he?"

He picks up on her last sentence:

"Hello you."

Shit – it's his voice!

"Ahm, hello..."

She's pulling a grimace at the way I said that, but my impromptu resolve to confront him is hanging by a thread already:

"I just thought I'd call you, hear how you are."

This is bad. This is really bad. She's shaking her head, then forming her hands into a megaphone:

"What she means is where the fuck have you been all the time!"

"Who's there?"

"No one."

"Doesn't sound like no one to me. Listen, I'm sorry I haven't been in touch, it's just that... It's a little hard to explain. How about dinner? How about tonight, in fact?"

"Yes... yes, that'd be great."

She has her face buried in her hands.

"Great. Nine okay?"

"Sure."

"How about the same place as last time?"

"Great, yes, see you there."

"See you."

She lowers her hands:

"Shit, honey, you really *are* in love. What the fuck was that?"

"I... I couldn't help it."

"Promise me not to forget to mention the torture you've been going through in the last few days when you're sitting opposite him, or I'll kick your arse when we see each other next time."

Most girlfriends I had in the last ten years turned out to be closet analysts, taking my life apart over flat-share dinners, over-interpreting everything. In the end, I always felt that I had been there for them, not the other way round.

Maybe that's why I've never felt a loss, not keeping up the kind of links other women my age seem to be keeping up, two-hour phone conversations on weekday evenings and Saturday catch-ups in neighbourhood cafés. But maybe – just maybe – I did miss something.

"Well, then, what can I say: I think you have a date. Need any styling tips?"

"I'll be okay, thanks."

"I know you will be. Girl oh girl: 'I just thought I'd call you, hear how you are.' I can't believe it."

"Shut up."

Maybe I missed someone who relaxes me the way the fashionista has relaxed me the last few days, someone I can be myself with, totally?

She leans forward and places her arms on the table that's in-between us, looking very serious, suddenly:

"I'm sorry about the other night."

"Sorry about what?"

"For the things I said about... for giving up, basically. I didn't really mean it."

"You didn't?"

"I've been thinking about it ever since. I'm missing you, and I'm missing the others. I'm missing... You know what I mean? But what I really mean is: We can't give up. That's what didn't let me go ever since I said what I said: We have achieved too much already."

I nod.

But have we really? The blockades have passed without a single consequence. That is, of course, if you don't count the draconian laws we're forced to live under now.

Hyper-security has been put in place around the entire parliament. Ruthless enforcers are patrolling the exclusion zone around the clock. No one is allowed to come even close to parliament any longer.

The feed has long started to concern itself with other issues again, and the mainstream media has reinstated our perennial financial crisis to the front page prominence we enjoyed for a few days.

In many ways, it's as though nothing has happened. Only that the sense of standstill feels even more definite, our helplessness even greater. *We might have lost more than we have gained.*

"But we need to find another way, I think. Something a little different. Something a bit more... female."

"Female?"

"Didn't I tell you? I've come to realise that it's going to be women turning this around. Men are not made for it."

"What?"

"They can't dream, honey. Isn't that clear? Whenever they try, their intellect scratches in. An intellect of vastly different qualities, mind you. And if not that, then the generally overrated organ that's dangling between their legs. But fun aside, look at them, out there. Take a real good look."

I nod.

"It's obvious, isn't it? The few who have taken steps in the right direction? Women! Seriously, I think this one's down to us, not them. That's what's going to happen. I've started to feel this, really, really strongly. You heard it here first."

"I kind of like that."

She leans back, pleased.

I'm biting my lower lip, but I told myself, before entering, that I would ask her – straight out. The picture in my head is turning too sharp to bear, the three of them.

Prepared.

"So, have you heard from him again?"

"Well..."

"Well?"

"I got another text, yes, but it's as cryptic as before. He's more interested in telling me... never mind."

"Telling you what?"

"Well, you know... how much he likes my eyes, and my lips, that kind of stuff. Anyway."

"Did you know him before, actually?"

With our We broken, I feel it's okay to break the unwritten rule of not probing our pasts.

"No... I mean, he's seen me once, I think. In my boutique. Quite some time ago."

"I see."

"The truth is, I'm scared, honey – scared of finding out what he really means. I'm not strong enough to... you know?"

"Isn't that –"

"Cowardly? Yes, but you have to understand how far I've come already. Half a year ago, all I was ever thinking about was where to party the next night. I lived between the dance floor and the boutique. I never thought further than the following day's hangover breakfast, and usually not even that far. I didn't even vote, didn't see the point. To be called political then – man, you would have sent me into a hilarious fit of laughter."

"Kind of amazing what has happened in here, yes... Have you heard from the leader or the brain, then?"

She shakes her head:

"You know I had this dream last night? I was driving this really fast car. Through the desert, or something. It was just me and this... carbon monster, and I could feel the engine and you know what? I fucking loved it. Can you believe it? A suppressed desire coming through, I guess? Made me think of, you know, a road trip. That would be something, wouldn't it? Man, the open road. Beautiful."

I want to tell her that I quite often have such dreams too, but I have a feeling that she only mentioned it to distract me, though I'm not sure from what exactly, so instead we just smile at each other and in that smile, everything else dissolves. *How about tonight, in fact?*

12

"Hallelujah."

"Too much?"

"No. Just very... sexy."

My quiet flatmate – barefoot and in a comfortable T-shirt – is standing in the door of her room as I pass through the corridor. It's true, the dark blue top I opted for has more cleavage than most tops I own, but I thought I had balanced it nicely with this light cardigan and the velvet scarf I'm wearing around my neck. My silver earrings might be counter-productive, but the trousers are jeans, a simple black.

I don't feel entirely myself, not fully comfortable, and that's the idea, exactly.

"Anyway, I have to hurry. I'm late already."

"A new date?"

"Kind of, yes."

I smile at her, trying to find my light black jacket from our overloaded coat hanger. When will we finally sort out a second one? Aren't we all equally annoyed by this situation?

There's the sound of keys, being turned, hectically, and then, there's what remains of her day's dose, a feminine freshness with a floral edge I can never quite identify:

"Good evening ladies. You're off? What a shame. I thought we could... you know..."

My head is inside our jacket jungle. Her voice sounds muffled:

"I thought... Well, I read this thing somewhere on the network this morning... about us being the in-between. We're the bridge. That's what makes it so difficult. It reminded me of you and what you said the other night. That's why I read it, I guess, and I thought... "

Where is that jacket? I'm fifteen minutes late already.

She keeps talking:

"Those that will come after us will have no choice. For them, this will be totally obvious. For us? It's different."

I pull my head back and stare at her.

"We're being asked to act, and, you know, act fucking drastically too – without seeing the consequences of our inaction. We have to change, not because we have to, but because we decide to. It's the hardest thing in the world, isn't it? I figured that's why I looked the other way for so long."

They are standing next to each other now, like sisters. My quiet flatmate is nodding:

"It's so easy, isn't it? To say: Let's leave this to someone else. Or at least to tomorrow. I didn't quite realise that, you know, elsewhere in the world, people do no longer have that luxury. And I feel bad."

I keep fondling. Everything speaks for looking away. Nothing speaks for the opposite. It's natural. Our bodies are telling us not to engage. That's why we don't want to see. That's why we don't want to hear, but I'm fifteen minutes late and I don't have time for this now!

"I've been thinking... Well, in fact, the two of us, we were talking about it on the phone earlier, weren't we?"

My jacket – finally.

"Yes. We were wondering if, you know, it might be possible for us to attend your meetings one night?"

"The... the meetings?"

13

What's left of them, now that the lights have been switched off? What's the bare room other than a bare room, now that the group is no longer going there?

Thinking of it now brings back memories of our early days, her red hair whirling around as she kept shouting at us that everything is political; that it's impossible not to be.

The fashionista, with her yellow sneakers on the table, suggesting that she might consider anger management classes.

Or the brain trying to explain, for the fourth or fifth time, that electricity cannot be stored just like that and how that's the biggest problem we face. Giant batteries, the fashionista shouted. Bring on giant batteries, I'll put one in our flat-share garden.

Occasionally, when I didn't take care and drifted off, even just a little, our voices seemed to blend into one; our borders no longer counted. That was a little scary at first – before I decided it wasn't. That's when it became magical.

I remember how the ex-banker used every chance he got to explain to the fashionista how his former profession was terribly misunderstood; how bankers were just human beings, too; how most of his former colleagues were further from the media's caricature than you could imagine – especially, of course, he, himself. He seemed so considerate, doing this. So thoughtful.

He was still *über-glad* he left the industry behind, though, he said. That's the word he used, stretching it like chewing gum: *über-glad, people.*

I will never forget the game he and the brain played for about a week, the brain suggesting to talk about growth, the ex-banker suggesting to fry a brain.

Or the leader – how she sometimes used our exhaustion at the end of a long session to launch into one of her dreary monologues about how we're not trying to become better human beings any longer; how in forty years all we really came up with is the network; how, at the same time, politics has decayed into whether we have a little more or less in the purse at the end of the month.

On more than one occasion, the fashionista actually fell asleep during one of those tirades, and I was close.

And then, sometimes, the leader just left – right in the middle of a session – for no apparent reason, and without explanation. She simply stormed out, at times mid-sentence, but no one ever raised an eyebrow. No one ever asked questions about it. Probably because she always came back.

Thinking of it now reminds me of the strangeness of those first weeks – the strangeness of this random group of strangers, meeting in a disused room, connected to the world by a tunnel alone. But, more importantly, the strangeness of me being there.

I will never forget the smiles on their faces when the leader brought me in for the first time. They looked as though they had waited for me. As though we had known each other a lifetime. Welcome, they said, welcome.

I can see myself, standing in the middle of that room in those early weeks, trying to play my role – a role.

It's a gradual process; I now know. I had to take an abstract issue – extremely far away, it seemed, both on a map and in my calendar – and bring it down to me. I understand this very well now: Everything had to become personal – deeply and disturbingly personal – rising temperatures and shrinking glaciers and the every-day reasons for it. Only then could I make the next step, and join them in their favourite slogan: That this is about all of us.

There can be no We in this unless there has been a painful I before; I know this now: If you don't make this about yourself first, the We is nothing but an empty phrase, entirely meaningless. For me, it was the most beautiful sense of unity I've ever felt in my life, and it all happened in a room with grey walls, two tiny windows, and no other furniture but a table and a few rackety chairs: I'm breathing like them; everyone's breathing like me.

It's only now that I understand what the bare room gave me all along – now I'm seeing it crumble. Entering it, night after night, felt like coming home in a way coming home didn't. The comfort I got out of seeing the others, the closeness I felt being with them – it all cumulated in what seems so painfully out-of-stock for me anywhere else, right now: a sense of belonging.

But I'm losing it before I even consciously noticed it was there. Unless, of course, we rebuilt the room, somehow... Unless I do?

14

"I'm still waiting."

He's looking at the white table cloth that's between us. The dark blue shirt he's wearing doesn't suit him nearly as well as his previous shirts have and I wonder if that's intentional, the way my outfit is.

He's not clean shaven either. He told me his facial hair doesn't grow very fast, so he must have been away from a razor for quite a few days, given the stubble I'm seeing. It all adds to the muddle that goes for his face tonight. For the first time since meeting him, it seems he's not quite sure what he's trying to say.

I called him an idiot for his behaviour and it hurt; I could see it. It felt good, too. It felt right.

My cheeks, like my hands, have stayed on my side so far. My uncovered arms are resting, calmly, beside my untouched, empty plate. There's no question who's more confident on this table-for-two tonight.

I grab him by his eyes:

"So?"

"I tried, didn't I?"

"You stammered something about something you had to be involved with, but I didn't understand it five minutes ago and I'm not understanding it now. As far as I'm concerned, that's not an explanation."

"You have to understand me."

"Do I?"

"I was hoping you would."

The look he's using to underline that statement is disarming the way his voice was when I called him earlier. Unfortunately, it feels genuine.

I look away.

The restaurant is bland the way it was last time round, but tonight I can feel it. There is no music, except that of other people, no real colour, except the red from our napkins. Ceiling, walls, the floor – everything has been painted in a lifeless nothing that tries hard to be taken for beige.

The two young waiters, wearing white shirts and black ties, are leaning against the counter at the small room's end, joking about whatever there is to joke about. Guests, probably.

"The real reason for my behaviour is a different one."

"I'm listening."

I return and it's as though pain has replaced the uncertainty in his eyes. He takes a deep breath:

"I'm crazy for you. I have been from the very first moment."

I stare at him, speechless.

"It's the truth."

I shake my head, losing focus:

"What can I say. It's nice to know that truth. It's nice to hear that truth, finally."

"But I told you about my ex-girlfriend, I told you about my desire for freedom, I told you everything."

I say nothing.

"I didn't want to get into anything for a while, nothing serious anyway. But then you came along and..."

He looks at his plate:

"And you invited me like no one has ever invited me before and there was nothing I could do. I was drifting in..."

"Drifting in? You were as much to blame, don't you think?"

"I wasn't in control. I shouldn't have led you on. I thought you would just be someone to spend some time with. But I realised my mistake. I should never have come that close to you, and I acted as soon as I did."

"After our last night."

"I tried to do what was best for us –"

"And what is this? If the psychoanalyst in you has so accurately identified what's best for us, then why aren't you sticking to your assessment, and see me instead?"

"I wanted to make good the damage, I guess."

"God, now you sound like... I don't need you to heal my wounds, okay? I'm a strong women."

I lean forward:

"Anyway, it's nice to see you. Despite, you know, everything."

I could have expected a smile in response to my unplanned advance; I could not have expected this overwhelming mix of relief and happiness. It's warmer than anything I have seen on his face since sitting down.

He seems to be clinging to these words as though something depends on them. Then:

"It's so nice to see you."

The smile I hand him in return brightens his face even further. Something has happened with it since I last saw him, and I don't mean the stubble, or the tiredness that has clustered beneath his eyes. What I mean is more specific, and yet more abstract at the same time: There's more weakness. There's more vulnerability. What I'm looking at is no longer the pretty facade I've been looking at for so long; there's more humanness. Looking at him like that, I feel, I can see deeper. That I can see more.

I wonder: Is this happening the other way round too? What does he see in me?

Intentionally or not, we have reduced the distance between us: One move – that's all it would take for our hands to touch. But I stay where I am.

One lapse – that's all it would take for my imagination to succeed and whirl me up into that sphere of my own making again, where what's being said on this table seems to be creating a new kind of unity, a more mature sort of bond, something much more solid than what has been there before. But I'm holding out.

I'm happy where I am – where we are – on this table, at a distance, where I'm no longer afraid to destroy anything, because, right now, there doesn't seem to be all that much to destroy. The heady excitement of those first few weeks has finally given way, it feels, to a much more realistic assessment of what we are to one another. In a way, I'm more relaxed than I've ever been with him:

"How's Freedomland then? Slept with lots of women in the last two weeks?"

"No."

"You're sure?"

He's looking away.

"Yes."

"I'm not sure you are."

I'm speaking with a jokey smile in my voice, but he doesn't respond.

"Let's be honest, eh?"

"Yes."

"What?"

"Let's be honest."

I grab his eyes as they come up again, and that's when the picture flashes into my head – just like that. As though it's been there for days, waiting:

"Tell me that's not true!"

It makes perfect sense: the timing, the last time I saw her, everything!

"Please tell me it's not true. You haven't slept with her, have you?"

"Who?"

"Don't play stupid, boy! Nice all that red hair, isn't it?"

Any resistance he's still clinging to is collapsing inside of him; there's no way of hiding it.

"You arse hole."

I'm standing before he can say:

"Look, I can... Listen..."

I'm walking before he can say anything else, past the middle-aged couple that has been eating a little more orderly next to us and past whoever else is eating or drinking or talking between him and the restaurant's door, which swings a little too far as I jerk it towards me, exiting with a bang.

The evening air hits my face, but not nearly as hard as I hoped it would.

I walk a few steps and lean against the coarse brick wall that's next to the restaurant's small front window, trying to breathe more evenly. A dim street-light shine covers the cars that are parked along this narrow side street.

Inside, the two waiters are probably laughing at me now. Or maybe they're laughing at him.

He might have his face buried behind his hands now. Or maybe he's grinning. Or maybe he's crying. Or maybe he's drinking from his wine as though nothing has happened, expecting me to return any minute now and sit down opposite him – re-composed – so we can talk about this issue like adults.

But then, he's standing next to me:

"I'm... I'm so sorry."

I'm not looking up. It might be fear or respect, but he's standing three steps away from me, in the middle of the pavement. People are passing between us, ignorant, uninvolved, careless. I stare at his polished black shoes.

"Maybe I have too much love to give."

I jerk up my head:

"That's just the worst thing to say! Where are you giving any love right now? Where? Tell me! Do you actually know what the word means?"

He doesn't answer. I push my hands away from the wall and cross them in front of me:

"In case you haven't noticed, I'm talking about something a little more than... whatever. Not something you can spread like Jesus in all directions, for everyone to catch some."

"I know."

"Do you? Do you really? Do you know anything?"

"Look –"

"Don't go look at me, okay? This isn't parliament."

"I'm –"

"Listen, don't try to explain this away in that cute intellectual way of yours, okay? You fucked her. It's that simple. Whatever. You're just like the rest of us. I wouldn't worry about it."

"What do you mean?"

"You did what you did for the reason we do things: Because, you know, we can. Anyway, whatever. Go inside and have the dinner you ordered. And have mine too. And..."

I push myself off the wall with both my hands:

"I have no idea if it's actually going to happen, but just in case – just so this is clear: *I* will call you, okay? If and when I want. Understood?"

"Understood."

15

In a front garden two streets down from our flat, there's a tree that takes my breath away every time I pass it, these days. Its crown – wide, narrow, in full bloom – looks like an elegant ladies' hat: Around its black branches, there's the fluffiest white, dotted with rich yellows and, here and there, a shade of light green. In fact, if it was a ladies' hat, I would be wearing it.

The tree I saw on the way here – a podgy trunk, wilful branches, a myriad of blossom-free twigs – was the opposite, but beautiful for different reasons. It concealed a dark tower block. If you're blossoming, I thought, they will all see you, if they come out onto their small balconies, on a clear morning, daring a look. What kind of tree it was, I have no idea.

At some point, I thought I might buy a book to identify some of them, but then, what difference does a name make? We're trying so hard to tag the world. To dissect, take apart, get to the core of everything. With this – the bushes and the shrubs being held, tenderly, by the darkness of a spring night – I actively don't want to understand.

The world has so much in stock for us in terms of the mechanic and the loveless – where else should we go, but here? Where it's wild. Where we don't understand. Where we are alone; my uncovered arms are on the rest of my bench, at the same angle on either side of me. The wood feels soft against my flesh.

I didn't bother to fetch my jacket or my bag when I left him standing in the restaurant's side street. Sometimes, your anger is all you need to stay warm. Even for the length of a night.

Down there, the city is still wearing its night-time robe. A dark veil covers the streets, the squares and the houses. Sometimes, when you're not asking for it, time loses its grip, and you float: Soon, the birds will start to wake from what I never had.

He texted around midnight – three hours after I had walked away, not turning around. Did it take him that long to find the right words, or did he seriously eat both our meals first, followed by a couple of drinks somewhere? Maybe both.

Strictly speaking, he has broken the rule I gave him, of course, but his words felt too important not to at least read them, and I have, five times so far:

It was so wonderful to talk to you again, he wrote. I can't tell you how much I've missed it.

I close my eyes and when I open them again, I see the day's skin – in a darkish blue now – and just beneath it, just atop the city's black spires, its quadrants and large cupolas, there's a lining, like satin, the colour of a pale rose that's withering *towards* more colour. The shyest hint of a new day.

I beg you for forgiveness, he wrote and got me to scroll down five carefully crafted pages to make me believe this grand and somewhat pathetic statement. Do I – believe him? I'm not sure. Do I – forgive him? I don't know.

He took my advice and didn't try to explain anything; instead: It's my greatest hope that we can move on together.

Down there, the city is starting to lose her robe, like a lascivious temptress. The robins have noticed, too.

He's still a penised piece of shit, of course, but the effort he's making to keep us talking tells me that he doesn't want this to be what it could, and maybe should be – the end.

The lining has turned tangerine. It's pushing its brightening shades higher and higher, slowly dissolving the blue, but I'm glued to the point where it touches my sleepy city. Its night-time lights seem but a fake imitation, compared to what has started to rise beyond its concrete constructions.

I haven't replied to him yet, and I'm not sure when I will, or how. My phone – which I had in my pocket, not my bag, when I left him earlier, an unwomanly habit paying off – is lying on my right thigh. Quiet.

My quiet flatmate kept it vibrating for almost an hour earlier, texting back and forth in both their names: Shit date, then? Well, yes, but.

It didn't take long for their sympathy to give way to what they were actually after: more answers.

I'm still not sure what, exactly, I did – almost unintentionally – when I gently turned their heads, taking their hands like my hand was taken also.

The polar bears, my outspoken flatmate said when I pushed past her earlier, leaving our flat for him, finally: I always thought this was only about the polar bears.

We'll help them along the way, I said, standing outside. Ready to leave.

But what you're saying, she said, is that it's about us, right? About all of us. What you're saying is that we must stop using the atmosphere as our rubbish bin. Did I get that right? A rubbish bin for our business-as-usual.

No one has ever summarised it better than that. From our doorstep, her quiet counterpart didn't sound quiet at all, suddenly: That's all nice and fine, she said, but here's what I don't get. If there really is an alternative to all *this*, then why the hell aren't we doing all we can to get there?

But that's when I turned the corner, and started running.

I understand now that, perhaps, it wasn't the issue itself that pissed them off, but the abstract, disconnected, preachy, apocalyptic way people – including me, probably – had been talking to them about it. Dreadful, but far away. Like cinema.

Did I take the issue out of its corner, or did I take them out of theirs? It seems they met in the middle.

The cinema, I can only assume, has started to feel a lot more like real life to them, and real life you can't just switch off or leave. Real life keeps nagging you the way they keep nagging me.

I imagined them sitting on our kitchen table, eagerly bowing over my replies as they arrived:

The meetings are over, I texted, but I have another idea. Keep tomorrow morning free.

Their okay came within seconds. Could they be the missing link? Tomorrow I'll find out.

I cross my arms in front of my chest and let my gaze drop to the ground in front of me.

I called the fashionista around two, or maybe it was three by then – who knows. She sounded sleepy, but who can blame her? She sounded something else too:

Why tomorrow? Why not next week?

Why not tomorrow?

She didn't answer that.

Are you up for it?

Why are you calling me this late?

Because.

Okay, well, I got to go.

Where to?

She didn't answer that, either.

Where are you?

But she didn't speak. I tried to listen more closely, but I couldn't pick up anything.

Why are you not replying? Where are you?

I'll call you tomorrow, okay? Or, I'll see you tomorrow morning. Whatever. Let's do it. Let's meet. I'll see you at the café, okay? I'll see you with your two flatmates, as you've suggested. Okay?

Okay. Any more from him?

No, she said.

Are you sure?

Yes, she said: See you tomorrow.

She lied to me, but it's too late to find out what, exactly, she lied about – and why.

A real signal. They are looking into my eyes and everything about them – the decisive look on the leader's faces; the brain's surprisingly upright posture; the way the ex-banker holds them together, like one – tells me that they are absolutely determined to go ahead with their radical action. Unless someone stops them.

I hug myself – tighter. Unless I do? My eyes, still pointed at the ground in front of me, lose their focus.

This isn't required, usually: No one haunts the streets of our cities anymore, asking uneasy, unwanted questions. We pick and choose from any shelf of any aisle – and if we don't like what we've grabbed, we go for something else instead. By now, our supermarket has a returns policy for almost everything. Right?

But tonight, someone *is* asking uneasy, unwanted questions. And I don't have answers.

I pull my feet towards me. Where do you draw the line? Not your friends. Not your neighbours. Not your parents. Not your sister or your brothers. Not your newspaper editorial and not your television talk show. Not your religious community, if you still have one. Not your society. You as a breathing individual. You as a human being; I as a human being: Where do *I* draw the line?

For hours now, I've suffered this ping-pong, wild fancies being battled down by reason, potential advances being played out against their damaging consequences, and no one heard me when I said out loud what I'm so terribly desperate for, up here: a voice of guidance. Someone to tell me what's right and what's wrong. The voice I fear won't come.

In a few hours, I will act.

After our meeting – as I've suggested: the fashionista, my two flatmates and me – I will not stop dialling their numbers until I have one of them on the line and then I will demand details. All the details. In a few hours – *after* our meeting in the café – everything will become clear.

I look up again. The lining – now it's the sky. It's as though one layer has given way to another, and it looks soft, and warm, like the skin of a lover you never want to stop touching.

A single bird takes off from the tree, its small black body pitched against this canvas in gold. I try to follow its erratic path for a minute, but then, it's gone.

If you agree to see me again, he said at the end of his message, everything will be different.

That was the bit I didn't quite understand, however many times I read over it:

I promise you. Next time we see each other, everything will be different. Extraordinary, even.

I shuffle on my bench. Soon, the streets will send their sleepiness down their drains. The parks will take their first breath, sending the ring-road flyovers into a stretch. House after house will blink, then wake, before lives will begin to spill out, filling our city with a new day. It's rising, like mist, from down below now, and I'm not refusing to be touched by its gentle claim... to be different. Maybe special. *Extraordinary, even.*

Four

Movement

"But here's the thing, right? What can we do? I just don't see it. I just don't."

My outspoken flatmate looks at me. She's feverishly twisting her dark brown curls when she's speaking, and when she's not. Everything about her baggy white outfit says weekend, no work. Her quiet neighbour, wearing one of her chequered shirts, is stirring her espresso without looking at it. She's nodding as though to say: My question, exactly.

I turn to the fashionista for help, but she's looking down, checking her screen like a naughty school girl would. Her legs – covered in black nylon from where the denim ends in frays – are pressed together tightly. Her white T-shirt looks as though she's slept in it.

She hasn't given me a proper look of acknowledgement since she arrived, twenty minutes late.

"I didn't come here with a ready-made answer, I'm afraid."

"Right."

The way my outspoken flatmate says it, I know this al fresco meeting is over already.

My fantasy to bring the four of us together didn't lose any of its intrigue walking down the hill and it didn't lose any of its intrigue during three hours of light sleep. I was fully convinced of its merit stepping into the shower, and I was fully convinced of its merit stepping out of the shower. All the way here, doubt was being beaten – by a dream.

Now I know it was a terrible mistake. No one says a word. Now I know I was wrong.

The fashionista, who has her eyes hidden behind oversized sunglasses, pours even more sugar into her cappuccino. One large gush. Two. Three. She puts it back on the table with much more force than necessary. Lifting her cup immediately afterwards, she spills froth on both sides. That's when I notice she's shaking.

Just before she joined us, it was my quiet flatmate who wanted to know why no one had made a film yet, showing exactly the kind of world I was telling them about – as though it existed. Not a story about that world, but one set in it. My outspoken flatmate agreed and said that seeing this would make a massive difference, and I imagined how, in such a film, people would have pictures on their walls of the politicians who took the really brave decisions way back. As heroes.

Stories do change things, my quiet flatmate said, don't they? The fashionista demanded to be introduced before I could voice my measured scepticism.

I open my mouth – to excuse myself and end this awkward situation, abandoning this doomed mission from a toilet seat – but before I can say anything, my outspoken flatmate leans forward:

"I was thinking something funny on my way here... Don't laugh at me, okay? But we don't think of ourselves as citizens anymore, do we? Maybe that's the problem?"

I stare at her. Not even the bare room dared to use that word. Not even our leader was brave enough to go there.

"I was thinking, you know: What's still binding us together?"

"Our GDP?"

"Oh yes, I forgot. The Greatest Domestic Penis. Us against everyone in percentage points. A bit pathetic, isn't it?"

"Pseudo, too. I mean, we're still only working for ourselves, aren't we?"

"Of course we're working for ourselves. Who else should we be working for?"

I turn my head at the fashionista, but she's watching equally entranced now. Neither of us dares to say a word.

"We're opening documents and we're closing documents. We stare. We're sending electronic files around the world without any idea where they are going and we can't quite see how it all connects. That's how I feel, anyway."

"Because probably it doesn't."

If this is slumbering inside them, is this slumbering inside all of us? Are we just not letting it out?

"Everything has become so individualised, right? So fragmented, I mean. It's that... I'm feeling we're not working *for* anything anymore, you know what I mean?"

"It's the game we play. But, I mean, we don't play it because we want to, right?"

They're both shaking their heads. There might be so much more in the air right now than I thought there was!

"We have a hundred thousand choices in this life. But that one isn't among them."

"Do you still vote?"

"What's the point? They're all dancing to the same tune, anyway. I should know. I work for the piper."

She laughs, but I suddenly see the ex-banker's face: My former colleagues are the real lawmakers now, he used to shout across the bare room. Isn't that obvious?

I had almost forgotten he and my outspoken flatmate shared this; she doesn't like to talk much about her job, usually. Good pay, but not much to say.

We didn't even ask for it, the ex-banker used to say. They surrendered their power voluntarily.

I quickly push him away, just the way I pushed away the brain. It was one of his favourite litanies:

The GDP? Even death, disaster and destruction count positively towards it. It's a charade.

The only thing that keeps me calm at this point is the government's repressive tendency: Security around parliament is still so tight no one will be able to come even close to a politician.

"You know, sometimes I think all we have learned is how to behave as consumers."

"Experts in economy stimulation, that's what we are."

"That's all we are, maybe."

"Empowered customers, yes, but where's the citizen supposed to come from?"

"No one taught me, that's for sure. All I was really told is how to be... flexible."

"Perversely mobile."

"Single-minded."

"And free."

The chosen regime makes its subjects – the sentence encloses my brain like tight plastic wrapping. A sudden silence engulfs our table.

It's as though this unlikely exchange is still sinking in, all of us talking over each other, across each other. It's as though we're still trying to find out whether our words were for real. I cross my legs.

Have we really just united over our very inability to do so? The lack of a shared interest has provided one. We are reaching out over the one thing we have left: our loss.

The chosen regime makes us what we are; what it wants us to be.

My gaze drifts off… Next to us, a few teenage girls are talking boys as though the world depended on it. Behind them, two elderly women watch in amusement. On our left, a beard is concentrating on his device, taking small sips without looking away from its non-reflective screen. Every face I see seems to be reflecting the late morning sun. It's so strong today, even I am spaghetti-strapped.

When I come back to our table, my two flatmates are looking as though to say: We said what, secretly, we wanted to say to someone for such a long time. Now, it's your turn. Now, you tell us.

I uncross my legs again. I reach for my cup. Everyone hears the gulp as the coffee runs down my throat.

"We could bring it all back, couldn't we?"

The fashionista!

"Think of the last few months. Think of what could happen if… The campaign is outgrowing its origins. Isn't that obvious? More and more people are joining this… effort. By the day. The usual suspects are being joined –"

"By people like us."

My quiet flatmate smiles like a student who knows she's given the right answer.

"By people who, not so long ago, wouldn't have dreamt about joining something like this."

"As citizens?"

"As whatever. As people."

My quiet flatmate nods. She's leaning forward now, tensely, with her arms crossed:

"Reminds me of my studies, actually, and it's true: Real change has only ever happened when lots and lots of ordinary people got together. You know what I mean?"

I didn't even consider how well they might fit into this.

"Exactly. Across all the divides we've become so good at creating for ourselves: nationalities, religious affiliations, the colour of our skin, economic realities."

"A little bit like on this table?"

I smile at her:

"A little bit like on this table."

I wasn't conscious of it at the time, but in the bare room, it seems, there was always something in the way.

What's your contribution, our leader used to ask me, always after they had all spouted theirs already. Maybe it had to do with me being the group's youngest member, the newly-arrived, but there was a sense of pressure, a tension, of sorts. Something I couldn't quite attribute to anything, or anyone, at the time.

Here, there's none of that. Here, we're all equals. Here, I feel, there's maybe even more to it – since I initiated us. I'm speaking with a confidence that has grown, almost without me noticing, but this particular change isn't about me, I feel, but about who's with me.

In the bare room, there was *her* – here, there isn't. Perhaps that's all there is to it?

"We need to turn this campaign, this effort, this whatever you want to call it, into... a movement, ladies. A real mass movement."

It's the fashionista, proclaiming this, but I'm seeing him instead. Giving *her* what he was meant to give me!

What we need is a movement that lives up to how complex the world has become, they are saying. But I'm still only seeing him. Kissing *her*!

What we need is a movement that tops every other mass movement that's ever been there before, they are saying. But all there is for me is their naked embrace.

Ever started a movement? Four women with ordinary jobs and ordinary lives, sitting on a café table on a Saturday morning, talking this through. That's a beginning, one of my flatmates is saying. They are hearing the sounds of a revolution, but all I hear is their fucking.

I'm clutching the cup that's still in my hand. I would be lying if I could, but it's back, and it feels different than before, the kindling that's the beginning:

I need to see you; I need to see you tonight!

"It's all there already. Believe me. All that's needed is a spark. One tiny little spark."

That, from the fashionista, brings me back, and it's almost a relief to hear my outspoken flatmate's trademark tone, making a measured return. She's back at twisting her hair too:

"But when it comes to this... I mean, we can't all turn into saints over night, can we?"

"Fuck that. There are no saints on earth. We're all just what we are. Right?"

The fashionista looks at me and I nod, but my quiet flatmate has adopted her neighbour's tone:

"I'm just scared that this becomes, you know... just another ideology?"

I shake my head. The fashionista:

"Have we done better in the last few decades without one?"

"I don't think we've lived without one. We've just stopped calling it by its name."

They nod at my assessment and my phrase crosses my mind, but before I can grab it, the fashionista leans forward, clutching her phone as though she's squeezing a lemon:

"You can take it from a hipster girl with an allergy to these kind of things: This isn't about ideology – that's just the lame label used by people who can't comprehend change that's a little more profound than the size of their tax bill. Their desperate self-defence, brand-marking our effort like that, just like they're sometimes brand-marking it as a pseudo-religion. Bullshit. As if belief had anything to do with it."

"The only belief that matters is the belief in our ability to change."

"Right."

"Right."

They're still sceptical and I can't blame them. They're still not exactly sure, but then, neither am I and neither is my neighbour, as far as I can tell. We're all in the same boat, and there's no point denying it. We're building this from scratch.

This isn't the bare room; there's no point denying that either. We're much calmer, less agitated and confrontational. There's less anger out here and, in a way, less energy. Or, perhaps, that's not right. Perhaps, it's just not as visible, not as obvious. Perhaps, it's running a little deeper. Perhaps, this is simply a little more mature?

I can't help thinking that what's going on at this table holds a much bigger promise than the bare room ever has.

Whatever is bouncing between us on this table – it's bringing back my urge to do something. Even better: It's bringing back my conviction that something *can* be done. There might be ways to achieve change we simply haven't considered yet. New roads will open up as soon as we start taking each other by the hand. Right?

I look around the table. My outspoken flatmate is leaning forward with her lips pressed together tightly. Her quiet counterpart has her hands behind her shortly-cut hair, elbows stretched out.

The fashionista is holding onto her chair's armrests, as though she's waiting to jump up any minute.

Looking at them – looking at us – I can't help thinking that something is about to happen with us, for us, because of us. Is this the next step? Are we? This We – the new We.

"It's easy for you, I guess."

"What do you mean?"

My quiet flatmate shrugs:

"You aren't caught up in most things we are caught up in. You're not so... bound. I can only speak for myself, but I still assess everything from, you know, my perspective. Which is my job, my city, this country. The particular position I'm in. And when we're talking about there being no borders and no limits and all that, then, for me, that's just abstract talk. That's what I mean. For you, it must be so much easier to see this."

My eyelids getting jerked up, violently – that's what it feels like. My nose being pressed against a glass door. And behind it, there's a picture I have not seen:

Everything I perceived as a terrible weakness during the last few months is turning into a unique advantage: I left the ballast of circumstance, the burden of a place, the limitations of a set environment – I come prepared. I left the dark alleyway of a national perspective, the distorting specifics of a particular position, the restrictions that come with staying put.

The layers I shed – were they nothing but sticky coating? Unneeded.

Everything I thought I had to fight with all my might is becoming my greatest ally in the wake of her words – and I'm not preventing the result:

I'm in a better position for this new We than anyone could possibly be.

"It's easy for all of us. Believe me. We can all get there. We just have to decide that's what we want. It's our choice. Yours, yours, yours and mine. It's all down to us."

And, in that moment, everything seems to fall into place. The peace flowing through us is my peace, this sense of being my sense. The hand I'm feeling is my hand and it takes me, gently, and whirls me up, further...

2

...and further, until it's all around me. I'm clutching the wood of my bench beneath my jeans.

From here, I'm seeing where our collective effort will take us.

In my pocket, my phone starts to ring. But the vibration it sends through my right leg isn't strong enough to beat the vibration that's going on in the rest of my body: From here, I'm seeing what's on the other side of the pain.

I take out the phone and press red. I don't even look at the display.

From here, I'm seeing what the radical changes we're afraid to make will result in.

Everything that's around me – the sprawling public transport system, the smartly-built homes, the energy that's being produced, where it's being used – is sharper than ever before, almost tangible, but it's in their combination that these elements reveal what has happened for them to come into place the way they have. A real re-think.

What seems unlikely now – from here, I'm seeing it for what we will all see it, once we're here: steps so inevitable it would be inconceivable not to take them, steps so obvious I can only ask:

How can we not do everything in our power to get here, where I am, now, already?

My phone – again. Red.

I left behind the technicalities and the feasibilities, the debates and their destructive detail, the scenarios, studies and their specifics. Step by step, stumbling blocks disappeared. Barriers dropped. Borders ceased to exist. I broke the unhelpful spell that has been imposed on us, everything being judged on probability, new ideas being dumped without a try, just because the figures don't match. I shook off the yoke of the what-is, our customary cannot-be-done – and this is my reward:

We created everything that exists – we can change everything that exists, too. I know this because I'm seeing it.

Everything is transitional. What we think of as normal today – seen from here, it's the strangest world I could possibly imagine.

Again. It's the fashionista who's trying to get hold of me. I hold her vibration in my hand.

From here, I'm seeing how we're shaping this world no longer as competitors, but as partners. What used to be others, elsewhere, has become the source for our shared responsibility; the language has changed.

Because the core has – the very core.

"What's up?"

"He's involved."

"What?"

"Your would-be boyfriend, ex-boyfriend, your whatever-the-fuck-he-is."

"What?"

My voice is so dry I can hardly speak:

"What?"

"And you're the only one who might still be able to stop him. There you go. I said it."

"You mean..."

What's been flowing through me refuses to leave – hope itself in a feedback loop, my conviction that something can be done in a chain reaction, empowerment powering itself.

"I mean: Get your arse to the parliament building as quickly as you possibly can."

My mouth refuses to cooperate. So does my mind.

"Are you still there?"

Her voice is trembling.

"He-loo?"

As the last remains of my high are vacating the space, her words come flooding in.

3

Here's what I wrote into my notebook before the hill started casting its spell, still processing everything we said to each other on our café table: Things *do* connect.

It's the sentence we left each other with, and I underlined the do as though to refute every moment of alienation I've ever felt in my life.

Think of our rights as women, I wrote, inspired by the fashionista, another battle we abandoned mid-way because a men-dominated world told us we had won it. Well, now the same men-dominated world is trying to tell us that it's all going to be just fine if we replace our light bulbs and recycle a little more.

The words I wrote weren't mine, but ours in their collision. What we arrived at together:

It's our shockingly inadequate what-is that gives all those profiting from it their voice, and they will continue to drown us out – until we start speaking with one voice. And snatch the what-is from beneath their shaking feet.

4

She told a lie, a sick joke. I'm still crouching in front of my bench, holding on to the cold wood.

Where I was sitting just a few minutes ago, my wear, and that of others, have turned it a little lighter. Up there, the backrest is covered in engravings, impulsive declarations of love and hate, amateurishly inscribed, misspelled.

My hands are gliding off, slowly; it doesn't make sense: Everything he told me about the issue – from the moment I helplessly asked him about it on our first table-for-two – speaks against it. All his words stand in the way. And then: the way he behaved inside the bare room! The way he treated the blockades!

On the ground behind the bench, a small bird is hopping, silently, in the sunshine. Above, they sing.

Sometimes, I tell myself that all the birds are singing just for me. When I hear them outside of my window, in the small hours, I imagine that they're telling me, in their sweet chorus, that I might not be able to sleep, but that there's no reason to panic. That everything is just fine.

And then, suddenly, they're all gone. From one moment to the next, there's utter silence, an unbearable nothing. As though they're pre-arranging these things, as though they're timing it all. From one moment to the next, they're off, collectively, to another tree, a distant garden, singing their song for another insomniac, falling on the deaf ears of a family, fully asleep, or a couple, arm in arm, lulled by sleep. The kind that has been reserved for couples, arm in arm.

You're the only one who might still be able to stop him. I push myself up. I start to run.

5

Aren't those who contributed least to our current situation suffering most?

That's what I wrote into my notebook too: Isn't our inaction already deepening poverty, spreading disease, fuelling conflict elsewhere? My quiet flatmate was so right about all this: Aren't we making worse what we so often claim to be making better?

That's the new We too. Because, I wrote, however hard we try to pretend otherwise, there are no borders in this. We got this down shockingly well: Every tonne of carbon dioxide we could save here, but don't, is a human rights violation elsewhere in the world. Already. And a little more so with every day that passes. With every hour. And, I wrote, isn't there enough blood on too many hands already?

Then I took down what my quiet flatmate said: If the sea is rising into your home, your food supplies are dwindling, and your fresh water is gone before you even saw it – I mean, what would you do? Build a loft extension?

6

"You have a superpower that makes cars go away?"

"No."

"Then I can't go any faster."

"Please."

My driver is tapping the steering wheel to whatever rhythm is coming out of his radio, happily humming: I have all the time in the world, baby, as long as my meter is on. On the other side of the window, bags bursting with Saturday shopping are being carried in both directions. They are faster than we are right now.

I touch his name – straight to voicemail.

I touch the leader's name – ringing. What has this snake done to him? *There was something I needed to be involved with.* How did she talk him into this? No answer.

I touch the brain's name – straight to voicemail.

I touch the ex-banker's name – cut off?

I touch his name again.

It's an automated message, not his real voice, announcing his unavailability, but it's still his voice in my head; it's still his words, streaming at me in a fragmented replay.

What if all the supposed cynicism was, in fact, his special brand of desperation? From the moment we started to talk about it on our first table-for-two...

What if his frustration wasn't really frustration, but pain? Skilfully concealed, like so many other things...

What if – ever since I first introduced him – he wasn't critical of the bare room's action, but our inaction?

What if he asked all his questions not to find out anything, but what he, himself, could do?

What if his disillusion with politics was so much greater than I thought it was? Did our idealism tip him over the edge?

What if his interest in this – and me? – had nothing but one aim from the beginning?

This. Whatever this is going to be.

I try the ex-banker one more time – busy? Who the hell is he talking to?

Fear is covering every muscle I have, like glue: Everything is happening in slow-motion, my phone sinking into my lap, my lids falling shut, my hands hiding my heated face, only to slither on their sweat, folding, prayer-style.

In my head, the sexiness of absolute conviction – a daring alliance of visionaries vowing to pay the price for changing the world forever – becomes, once again, the madness of fundamentalism. The scary implication of making the bending a breaking gives way to a mesmerising romanticism. Noble, selfless acts that could benefit all of us, equally, morph into crazy whims – and back. Courage is being debunked for what it also is, before a new bravery wins it, once again.

I want to switch tabs, log off, sign out; I'm looking for an option that isn't there.

"Please. I need to go faster."

The driver turns his stubbly white face back at me in a wry smile:

"Don't we all need something, darling?"

I grab the handle and jump out without looking what's behind me.

7

That's how it connects too, I wrote, approaching carefully what was said. Slow-writing every word:

Are we just going to lean back and smile when our lifeblood runs out and we haven't put the alternatives in place? Are we just going to accept our loss when changing circumstances block us from what used to be within easy reach?

I paused, but then I exploded: Let's not kid ourselves! We're going to claim whatever we can claim and it's only a matter of time until some of us will start to make that argument not with words, but – I didn't finish the sentence. Instead I wrote across two pages:

As for those still calling themselves peace activists, don't they have to be with us now too?

And we? Aren't we all peace activists now?

I looked at this page for a long time: The new We – isn't that the peace movement of our generation?

8

And then, there's others. Random figures, put, as you would for a board game, a few at first, then more. I can't make out their faces; their bodies appear unreal to me. I can't make out their position, or mine. The street is a central street, the city my city, and I'm here – on this corner, in this country, of this world – but I'm not sure what it all means any more.

I walk on. My lungs are taking in air – the fumes from exhausts and the stench from overdue rubbish bins and whiffs of sweat and perfume – but nothing seems to come out anymore.

My eyes are registering vague outlines – the pavement's grey below and the sky's ridiculous blue above – but nothing else seems to arrive, not the shapes of the buildings that line the street to my left, or the cars that are passing me on my right. Not what's still ahead of me, or what I left behind.

There's blond hair and there's black hair and there's brown hair, but there are no faces to go with it: Everyone is walking in the direction I'm walking in.

Thirty, forty, fifty – I don't know. They've started to join this from side streets now.

That's when I notice the uniforms. They're standing in small groups everywhere: on corners, in front of shops, between parked cars. I'm not sure whether it's uncertainty, reluctance, or simply their order, but they're not moving. They're merely watching.

I walk on – faster now. The crowd has become so dense other bodies are brushing against me.

A white polo-shirt, a jeans jacket, a black top. They are surrounding me, a hundred or maybe two, three, four. A dark blue suit, a black hoodie, a flower dress. I look left and right. A working man's glaring yellow, a heavy-metal jumper, a blouse with butterflies all over it.

I turn my head around, but they're right behind, eyes ahead. Who are these people? And what do they want? Whatever fragments I can catch, I can't hold. The sounds surrounding me – human voices, car horns, the distant beating of a drum – blend, cancelling each other out. Leaving nothing.

My hands come up against a teenage top, my nostrils lost in her overindulgence of hair products. A lower arm touches my naked shoulder from behind, its hair ticklish, before it's gone. We stop, because we have to.

I raise my head, as she recomposes herself in front of me, but all I see is people. Everywhere. This procession has come to a halt. I can't walk on.

Do these people have any idea? Don't they know that I'm the only one who really needs to get there?

But I'm halted, like everyone. What's happening at the end of the street means more to me than it can mean to anyone, but there are no gaps in this crowd. There's no way.

"I need to... please...."

I'm shocked to hear my own voice, not to see her contempt: Don't you have eyes in your head, sister?

Yes, but don't you understand? I'm the only one who can still stop him! And it's now, or never: I push her aside, and then I push aside her spiky-haired friend too.

"Are you fucking crazy?"

I press my arms against my chest, as tightly as possible, and start slipping through, eel-like.

"Fucking crazy."

Their squeaks – sounds. Their faces – masks. Their bodies – nothing. Because he is everything. *The most wonderful thing that has happened to me in years.* Because he is all that counts right now. For me – and for them too. Don't these people understand a thing?

I press on, and nothing else registers – not the sirens that have started to swell in the distance, not the helicopter that is circling overhead, not the frantic voice that's coming from a megaphone, somewhere ahead.

Instead, his soft lips are beginning a smile. They have just touched mine for the first time. I'm crazy for you. I have been from the very first moment. Our noses are in a tender touch. His warm, naked breath strokes my closed eyes. And then, his outstretched hands lead me away – into our world. The one we create for ourselves.

Her elbow stings my stomach, before two broad backs stop my advance. I detach my hands.

A nose is being pressed into my back from behind.

"Please! I need to get there!"

But I'm locked in.

I bang my hand against whatever is in front of me now, but it doesn't help: He's slipping away from me just as we reach the door to our world. Gone, forever?

I press with all my might, but the movement, when it comes, is not on this street. It's so unusual, I don't know where to locate it at first. I move my hands towards my chest. Through the sweat-soaked fabric of my red top, there's this sped-up rhythm, my own feverish drum, but it's not the beating that's wetting my eyes. Knees are hitting my legs, shoes are trampling my toes. I press my hands tighter against the red.

What I'm feeling isn't the beating; what I'm feeling is the burning.

9

When the grip loosens and I regain my senses, I can hear the voice of a child:

"I can see a long line, Daddy."

"Of what, darling?"

She must be on his shoulders next to me. My blood is pounding against my temples.

"Of police. They're standing like stone. It goes all around the building. I think."

The exclusion zone they put in place after our blockades. No one is allowed to come closer to the parliament than that. It's where we end and they begin.

"What's the other way?"

"People, Daddy. More people than I've ever seen in my life."

I'm bent forward, with my hands on my knees, staring at a pair of premature flip-flops, leather plimsolls and shiny white running shoes. The crowd has loosened up, ever so slightly. People are standing the way you would for a rock concert now.

Only – where's the stage?

I don't dare to look up, don't want to see. I wish I wasn't here, wish this wasn't me. Those around me have become a menacing hum, overhanging the concrete like smog.

I slide my hands up my jeans, rising carefully, staring at my black sneakers. With my hands pressed around my waist in a vain attempt of self-protection, I start straightening my neck, slowly travelling up a nervous pair of legs in front of me.

The moment the flesh turns to fabric, the crowd erupts. My head jerks up at once.

No more breathing.

No more blood.

But I'm behind the curtain, all of a sudden, in the arms of my mother, weeping and repeating that I didn't want this, never wanted this. That I love her, love her more than anyone in the entire world. That it was all a mistake, a terrible mistake.

And my dad takes my shivery hand and puts it in his, and in the background, there's music playing, music I know, and then my sister is there too and then – is this really happening? – we're all looking down my hill *together*.

Because I'm pointing them there. My mum and my dad and my sister are seeing what I'm seeing, from here, and it's taking their breath away too: Have we really stopped doing what we're doing commanded by the ghostly forces of our Now? Did we really manage to shift our priorities in a way we would never have thought we could? Have we really turned things upside down – perhaps the way they were always meant to be?

Down there, the rivers flow in silence. Down there, the trees no longer moan, and they're cheering! My mum and my dad and my sister are applauding what they're seeing from here!

It takes me a long while to realise it's actually happening around me.

I rub my face with both my hands, but the applause is real and it's here. And so am I.

The cheering is all around me, but there's nothing where I'm looking. Even on tiptoes, I can only see heads, before they stop, abruptly, coming up against the line. Beyond, there's nothing. The parliament building is quiet against the sky's blue, its features glistening in the sun.

I turn left, right, left, and that's when I realise that no one is looking where I'm looking. Their heads aren't raised, but lowered; it's the same for everyone: all eyes are down.

My fingers slide into the pocket of my jeans. The password leaves four stains of sweat.

Then I'm holding it in my hand too:

#insideparliament.

I'm scrolling back in time – half an hour, an hour, an hour and a half. That's why there are so many people here! The feed has been wild with hints and rumours for almost two hours. One tap returns me to the beginning: The latest link, maimed into incomprehensibility, only started appearing a few minutes ago. Whatever it is, this must have caused the screaming. I tap, but my phone is unusually slow.

A voice rises as I look up, glancing at those around me, staring at their displays, aghast, bewildered, spell-bound:

"I must ask you to stay calm, please."

Her words are coming through a megaphone, from somewhere not too far, out of the line:

"Please. Stay. Calm."

I look back at my screen, where the page has come up, and that's when I understand. That's when I see. But I'm neither clapping, nor am I staying calm.

10

The new We, I wrote into my notebook, that's us, getting ready to walk. I bolded every letter: WALK.

Our café table – once the fashionista had stormed off to the ringing sound of her mobile – reminded me of the triangle I had first seen in the bare room. I saw politicians, companies and the people, but this time round, I saw something else – because we didn't point our fingers; we didn't even argue.

We reached out.

That's when I realised where our café meeting was leading us. Picturing the triangle, I saw what we'll have to do, all three of us: Take a step forward.

Politicians, companies and the people – what we'll have to do is walk towards each other, and break the deadlock with our own feet. WALK.

This, I felt, was *my* way forward, what I've been looking for ever since I first joined the group.

There was only one problem: I had no idea what this walking could look like.

11

I move the picture closer to my eyes. It's shaky, but not because of the camera; the camera is static.

It streams every parliamentary debate, even the most minor and uninteresting ones, straight to the web, in a single-frame, without comment, in real-time. A government initiate for more transparency transmits the centre of power into my hand – and into all those hands around me.

My left hand, still around my waist, tightens. My fingers pinch as hard as they can: How could I have been so blind when this must have been so obvious!

The camera shows the scene in a beautiful symmetry. In the frame's centre, it rises – silently but potently. It's the best symbol they could have picked.

I shake my head; it made sense all along, didn't it? Only I didn't see it. Only I didn't understand.

It's almost self-evident – to combine the bare room's growing conviction that power needs to be pushed, if it is to be moved in the right direction, with what only he had: access to it.

I'm looking at the exact spot where, day after day, inaction is being sold as action. Where stagnation is being excused in broad sweeps of polished rhetoric.

But today, no one has stepped up there to say a word. Today, the movement has.

The two of them are both sitting to the left and to the right of the stand, with their backs against it.

His horn-rimmed glasses do nothing to hide the nervousness that's all over the brain's face. There's so much in his facial expression I would like to decipher, but I can't get myself to linger on him for more than a moment, given who's on the other side. And with him, it's not nervousness; with him, it's something else.

I look away, hastily. Around me, fingers are feverishly tapping tapping tapping. Everyone is keen to be the first, I assume, determined to deliver the best frontline account, the one dispatch that will make it through. *#insideparliament* must be on fire, the feed on the brink.

I look at him again. His arms are stretched back, so his hands meet the brain's on either side of the stand. From their elbows onwards, an angular metal tube unites them. Their legs are stretched out flat on the ground, each man's feet in their own chains.

The two of them are bound, inseparably, to what's in-between them. Even if they wanted to – they can't move.

The fashionista's hand on my shoulder becomes a familiar embrace before it has a chance to hit me as a shock. She keeps holding on, her arms flung tightly around me, as though she wanted to say something with her physical closeness.

Her head is tilted, slightly; my shoulder feels that she has her lips pressed together tightly. I loosen my grip, but her hands won't let go of my back.

I look at her, with my arms still around her waist, but her eyes don't make it across my tummy.

"How... How did you find me?"

My voice – croaky and weak – sounds like that of someone else. Unused for a decade.

"I figured you'd be as close as possible."

She keeps her eyes down, but her face doesn't leave any doubt: Can't we just hold on?

She leans her head against my shoulder:

"I'm sorry, honey."

"Sorry?"

"I didn't give you a chance and I'm sorry."

This – the word sorry, I assume – allows her to look up. Her eyes are even redder than this morning.

"You knew, didn't you? All along."

"Last night. Only last night! But it doesn't matter anymore now, does it? I mean, we're here."

"How... how did you find out?"

She has taken out her phone and is looking at the picture we're all seeing: The man who intruded our group has intruded his own home, evading one of the most sophisticated security operations in recent history, tricking them all. It's a brilliant coup if ever there was one.

She doesn't look up:

"Isn't that obvious?"

"You couldn't stand his messages any longer?"

"That too, maybe, yes, but..."

"Did you... I mean, did he..."

"I thought it might make him talk some more."

I stare at her.

"Fuck, okay, that wasn't the only reason, probably. I felt... It was very nice too. It's funny, but I've started to see something in him that... Anyway, he did talk."

"But where is he?"

"Further towards the back of the crowd."

"I don't understand."

"He was never part of anything."

"What?"

"The messages to me – that was just his wishful thinking. The street guerrilla in his head."

"What?"

"Hilarious what some people do to get a girl into bed, isn't it? Anyway, he got a call from the brain yesterday. Sounded all nervous and shit, the thinking man, and, well, he said a little more than he should have said, probably. It wasn't that hard for us to put one and one together, after that."

"So how... I still don't understand."

"The ex-banker met your man once, shortly after our last full meeting. He refused to talk about it yesterday, but I think your man gave him the cold shoulder over, you know, his particular idea of getting radical, and it's not something he's very good at handling. Hurt pride, you know what I mean? How these two got together, I have no idea."

She nods at her screen. The text message the brain got in the bare room. The one he didn't want me to see.

"I think I have a pretty good idea. No space for cold shoulders when things fit so beautifully. And if I hadn't been so blind..."

I can see this very clearly now: What stayed obscure to me did so because, secretly, I wanted it that way; the fog of uncertainty was the fog of fear. My picture – the three of them in a row that didn't mean a thing – was nothing but a cheap excuse. Not to answer the unfamiliar question.

"What about her?"

The fashionista points at my screen instead: The brain's lips have started to move.

"She's a different story."

I look closer: The nervousness on his face is all but gone; there's only his conviction now.

"No one has heard from her since the blockades failed. We have no idea where she is."

"What? Seriously?"

"Check the feed, honey. They have his words."

I switch tabs:

We have come here today, because we have to.

Without another word, she puts her arm around my shoulder. I put mine around her waist. We're both looking at our own screens.

And we are determined to stay where we are until someone steps in-between us...

I don't need a camera to see the brain's face. The crowd is cheering my doubts away: These people aren't here to watch; they are here in support!

...switches on the microphone and announces to the world that this country is taking the steps that need to be taken.

Chained to the heart of power, the brain is delivering our message, almost word for word:

We believe that you have it in you to make history on the grandest scale today.

I don't need to be inside the building to be with him – and neither does anyone else out here.

And we won't leave until you do so.

We're holding hands by holding our phones: *#insideparliament* means we are the feed; the feed – that's us.

This stage is set for you.

We're a twenty-first century congregation, the network in flesh and blood – and we won't go away either.

Our demands are as follows.

I turn my head at the fashionista. I remember how bitterly we fought over those demands. How we quarrelled over every word, discussed every comma. It took us three weeks to sign off what's filling the screens now.

"You think she's okay? Our leader, I mean."

She doesn't look up:

"I wish I could say yes."

They are, even now, some of the most memorable scenes from the bare room, our leader banging her fist on the table, insisting that any demand on fossil fuels would have to come with a pledge for those who dutifully served our advancement up to here. They deserve dignity, not punishment for a position that isn't their fault, she shouted into the ex-banker's sarcastic laugh: What about the dignity of those working in the car industry? How about a fund for stewardesses? What about ex-bankers, for that matter?

The fashionista in her passionate defence for shopping – it's about doing it differently, about wasting less, about a new kind of creativity, she said with a spark in her eyes. Only to hear from the brain that, if we aren't serious about the reduced lifestyle, we have no right to demand anything from anyone at all.

The three-hour argument that had the ex-banker and the fashionista on one side of the room – Efficiency incentives will kick-start a race of innovation! – and the brain and the leader on the other – More efficiency will only serve as an excuse not to change what really counts!

At the end, we had three fine-tuned paragraphs – a fair and binding global emission regime, the radical restructuring of our antiquated energy systems, and effective efficiency laws – and maybe it's the collective sweat that went into these sentences, or maybe it's the fact that for every contentious point we did, in the end, reach a consensus – but, for me at least, it's as though these demands come straight from the heart.

And the brain has just delivered them to the world:

The stage is yours.

I switch back to the static camera. The brain has his head bowed now – submissive, but with dignity. As though to say: This isn't about us, but about you. I still can't believe he is the one, doing this – of all group members: the brain. I wish they were here now too, the ex-banker and our leader. I wish we could watch this together.

"You would have stopped him, wouldn't you?"

She's looking at me now.

"Who?"

"Your ex-boyfriend, silly. Your would-be boyfriend. Your boyfriend. The man on your screen."

"No, I wouldn't."

"Yeah, right."

"Yes, I would. Yes, I probably would have stopped him..."

"Or at least talked to him, which might have been enough for him to reconsider. And I didn't want that to happen, because... Because look at your screen!"

I nod:

"You probably did the right thing."

"I don't think there was a right thing. I feel terrible for not having given you a chance, but I would have felt terrible otherwise too. There was no way for me to win."

She pauses:

"But in the end I also figured: If he's prepared to take a risk like this, how serious can he be about commitment to you. Or anything. Right? Honey? Right?"

I stare at her:

"So... you don't believe this is going to work?"

She turns at her screen:

"All we can do is watch, right?"

I don't know where it has been hiding until now – behind my relief that this isn't, after all, what I had feared, probably, or behind the feeling of strange pride that filled me during the brain's delivery – but it's hiding no longer. Fear is preparing its armada for a full-on attack, I feel the panic in all my veins: It's him, in there!

I pull her closer to me. Will this government have the audacity to do what no other government has done before – and set a precedent of hope? Will this government be the first domino in a long row of governments around the world doing the right thing?

Nervousness traverses the crowd. I can hear more sirens now. Somewhere, there are shouts.

Whatever will happen to him and me – it's no longer his choice, and it's no longer my choice, either. Whether we like it or not, our future is now in the same hands as everyone's. Theirs.

Whatever will happen is being decided in the same back room where they must be wording their response to this right now, and whatever they will come out saying will decide where we're going. The two of us, and all of us.

But the stand remains empty. No one has stepped up to say anything.

"Honey, what's happening?"

She switches back to the feed for an answer as to why the crowd has just erupted in excitement.

"Shit. You might not want to –"

"What?"

Too late. I have seen her screen.

"The link's on the feed."

My arm is sliding away from her. As though to grant me my privacy, she takes hers off my shoulder. I'm holding my phone with both my hands now.

The new video is being streamed to the blog of a junior minister in the environmental department, and he's probably breaking the law, filming in there like this, but so far, no one has stopped him. He knows how to use his zoom, too: The frame is filled, perfectly, with a single face, and it's piercing me, where touch is rare. Where it really, really hurts.

I bring you closer.

The picture is so sharp, it's as though you're sitting opposite me, just the way you did, on that first table-for-two, remember?

Remember – us? I move your soft, sensuous lips closer to mine. You look like you know I'm looking.

I'm right here!

All sorts of voices are saying all sorts of things around me, but I hear nothing.

What do they know? Nothing. But I understand – about your independent streak and how you have suppressed it for too long. About the drug that's been circulating through your body in the last few weeks. That you're doing this for yourself, too: You might be in chains, but this is the greatest moment of freedom you've ever felt. Isn't it?

I know that you haven't asked anyone about this. Not your former girlfriend. Not your family. Not me. I know that you're spurned from somewhere deep within, and it might give you everything you have been looking for. Please say so.

The entire world is watching as you fix yourself – and it could be all that's needed. *It might take some time, or it might happen very suddenly.* The fashionista's words are dancing around my head. Please tell me that this is all that's needed. *When he's realising what's at stake.*

"The static camera has gone black!"

It's the fashionista's voice, from behind me, but I don't turn around.

"What the hell is going on?"

Forget the others; think of me! Think of what we had, of what we have! Let them all change tabs, move on, go away; they have no idea what's happening with you, anyway. I know this should have happened so much earlier, so very differently, but this is the only chance we have left: I am ready to admit everything I haven't admitted to you, say everything that hasn't been said. Please.

No one else can see what I can see. No one out here has a clue what's happening inside of you, but I can see it in your eyes. I can see it so clearly. Please say it; please just say it.

The first wave presses your lips against my breasts, the second sweeps me to the right.

I grab the fashionista's arm, but my hold doesn't endure the crowd's current: My fingers are touching hers before they lose each other at their tips. We're being swept in opposite directions, her voice fading with her:

"Honey – what the hell is happening?"

I trip, grabbing for hold – in vain. A hand pulls me up, but when I turn, she's gone.

The crowd is moving in a collective swing now, as though someone was gently rocking us. But there's nothing gentle about faltering legs, clutched hands, squeezed lungs. It's happening everywhere.

Screams are rising, and falling. Like sirens.

My feet are no longer listening to me, but to the current that's sweeping us back and forth. They know resistance would be fatal: I have to go with the flow, however brutal the flow will get. Back and forth. Back and forth.

My arms are no longer listening either. Coming up against someone's shoulder, they bring my screen towards my eyes again and that's when I see that the streaming minister's camera has been turned.

Instead of him, there are about ten of them now, maybe fifteen. They are scattered, like a school class with half its students missing.

The mass around me is shaking the picture I'm holding, but I can see three women, all of them in the front row. They are leaning forward, with their hands in their laps. Tense with anticipation. Can this be right?

I grab the shoulder in front of me with one hand, holding myself up that way.

There's no anger. These politicians are being targeted on what could have been a quiet Saturday, and there's not even a hint of annoyance on their faces. The trained compassion, the perfected empathy – there's none of that, either. And it's in everyone.

The moment I understand – they don't know they're being watched! – the shoulder in front of me surrenders. I saw what they're hiding, usually!

I stumble forward, clutching my phone, but within seconds, other bodies have filled the vacuum.

I raise my arms in compliance, lifting their unexpected expressions into the sky.

For a moment, I saw these women and men for what they really are – breathing just like me. I saw fathers and I saw mothers. I saw sons and daughters. And I saw their pain. The distress on their faces reminded me of everything he tried to explain to me about what it means to be a politician, these days, but when it was just words then, now it's people.

The crowd doesn't let me lower my arms. I'm gasping for air that doesn't arrive.

For a moment, I saw these politicians trapped by a system that doesn't allow them to do what their human hearts tell them to do. By a system we, ourselves, created.

An elbow drills into my stomach; from face to face, I saw them for what we all are – if only I could look again! – slaves to our chosen regime.

The moment the phrase arrives, gravity loses its pull, my eyes their sight, my mind its control.

I'm being flushed forward in a freak wave of helplessness, my arms squeezed against my pounding chest, my legs pressed together tightly, and all I still see is:

We created everything that exists. All I still see is: We can change everything that exists.

All I've gathered on my hill is still with me, but they don't hear me, do they? They are far away, inside there, unconnected. No one hears me:

Our regime isn't self-evident. No one hears: We can choose differently.

My shoulder is first. Then, my knees. Then, my entire body is being pressed against the barrier.

It doesn't move. Body against body against body. It's impenetrable.

But the crowd in my back keeps pushing.

"Stop. Please…"

I feel my racing pulse throughout my body, feel every desperate breath I draw. Somehow, I manage to push my phone into my pocket, but having two hands in my defence doesn't help: They're squeezing me... further... towards blackout.

And the barrier doesn't give. Not an inch. Blood floods my brain. My stomach turns.

"Stop... Please..."

Bur they are pushing me *up* the barrier now. My hands are sliding towards the space that's between their heads of stone, their eyes hidden behind black visors, the last hint of humanness concealed, perfectly.

The pressure brings on a violent flickering that doesn't stop when I shut my eyes. I grab their shoulders.

My insides are being squeezed up my throat, into frantic flashes of white. I have my elbows between their visors now. Wetness spreads behind my lids.

I retch. The flashes are slowing down. They're paling out. They're losing all their life...

But then I pull.

Using all the strength I have left, I pull like I've never pulled in my life.

The pain traverses my body as my shoulder hits the ground on the other side. This has happened so quickly I wonder if it has happened at all. I lift my head, slowly.

I see their heavy boots from behind. Even if they wanted to, they can't turn around. What they're making up doesn't give them a chance: Even just a small gap in their ranks would see this area flooded with people.

There's the smell of leather, and of whirled-up dust, and there's the smell of blood too.

It takes me a while to realise it's my own. The graze covers my upper arm, but the graze is not where the pain comes from.

I turn my head the other way. Between here and the building, there's nothing. The police have surrounded the centre of power with a vacuum, and I'm inside of it, lying on the zone's concrete ground. At its far end, a single police van stands parked, its blue lights flashing expectantly.

I place my right hand next to my body, all fingers stretched out. Small pebbles bore into the flesh. My face contorts without my control as I start pushing, contracting all the muscles that are listening.

I pull my legs close, steadying what is now almost an upright position. My left arm feels numb; it dangles from a swelling shoulder like a limb.

Where I am, the crowd sounds muted, like a television that's in another room. It's an indefinable drone, out of which screams rise, like fountains, every few seconds or so. Their boots are unmoved, the barrier doesn't give: Orders are orders. But the screams I hear are screams in pain.

I bend over, moving my balance onto my knees and, using my unharmed side, push myself in a kneeling position, my back facing theirs, my view of the zone. The van's back doors have been opened, I can now make out.

Then, in one swift move, I rise up. The dizziness traverses me in a single swell, until all I'm left with is the shakiness of my legs.

But I am standing. My arms are dangling from either side of my body. I use my right hand to bring up the left strap of my top, careful not to touch the graze.

Is our anger organising? I try to concentrate: In my back, individual voices seem to be coming together in a chant. I can't make out the words from where I am, but there's no doubt: We are rising in volume. Are we gaining strength?

Maybe it's the confusion that's started to wrap me, like a cloud, from the moment I looked up from the ground, or maybe it's the pain, or maybe it's simply that there doesn't seem to be any another option, but I start to walk.

Are we gathering all our courage?

My steps are tiny. I can hear the concrete beneath my shoes. My feet are hardly lifted. Every slurp twitches through my swelling shoulder, spreading from there.

The crowd fades away, slowly, as I leave the barrier for the emptiness of the zone, trying to make my steps bigger, trying to raise my feet a little more.

I'm almost half-way in when I see them, at the far end of the zone. They're maybe ten of them, or maybe fifteen, split into two groups. They seem to be walking almost as slowly as I am walking. Towards the van's flashing blue lights.

It takes me another few steps to realise what's at the centre of each group and then few more to understand what it means. In my back, someone is shouting something I don't understand. It's coming from this side of the barrier.

I walk faster. Their legs are still in their own chains, their arms in police handcuffs.

The brain is first. There's a hand around each of his ankles. Another two officers are carrying his upper body, one holding him beneath each arm. I wonder if he's watching, or if he has his eyes closed, his thoughts in such a moment for no one but himself. There's nothing anyone can do for him now. The van is too close. It's too late.

I jerk my head at the second group. Whoever is shouting in my back is catching up.

He's being carried the same way. Like the brain – who's entering the van now, I can see at the edge of my vision – he doesn't speak, doesn't complain, doesn't resist any of what's happening to him. Unlike the brain, the man who didn't finish saying what he started to say has his head raised, ever so slightly.

Without a second thought, I start to run.

"Stop at once!"

A male voice. Behind.

"Stop!"

Startled, his group stops. They're looking in our direction now, seeing me first – a strange apparition, limb-armed, running through the emptiness of the zone – and then him, just behind:

"Stop if I you don't want to get shot."

That's when his head raises further – I'm here; I'm right here!

"You have to stop immediately."

Behind.

"Stop now!"

Ahead. But I keep running. He raises his chained hands, but they push him down, forcefully. I keep running.

"Freeze. Now!"

They pulled them, almost simultaneously, one of them standing to his right, the other one standing to his left, framing his face with their pointed muzzles.

I can see your eyes, can you see mine? Finally, there's no screen in-between, and everything I saw on your face is still there, even though it's framed by their guns, but there is so much more, and your lips are moving. There's so much more:

You.

What are you saying?

The sting almost knocks me out. Tears shoot to my eyes. A harrowing scream echoes through the zone, as though those buildings were mountains. The officer has grabbed me from behind.

I can't hear you!

What are you saying? Both my arms are crossed behind my back now. I'm bent, gasping for breath: I need to hear you!

The two officers lower their guns, slowly.

Please.

The metal is cold around my wrist, but I'm clinging to your lips. I'm desperately holding on: I'm still here!

And, then, just before I'm being jerked around, you say it again, your chained hands raised before they get pushed down again, and this time, I'm reading your every word. This time, I'm seeing every syllable on your face.

I wail, pointing my chin at my shoulder and the officer loses his grip on that side:

"What on earth were you thinking?"

He inspects me, shaking his head: Clearly a mad woman! But his disdain doesn't touch me.

"I just needed to... hear. I just needed to... Please take me away, okay? Just take me away."

He points at the barrier.

"That's exactly what I'm doing."

I hear the thudding of a door, and then another. He leads me away, slowly.

Ahead of us, the barrier stretches across my teary-eyed vision. Seen like this, the zone's concrete looks like a shore that's giving way to the sea in a brutal contrast, human waves constantly splashing against the uniformed cliff. I can hear them now again, roaring ferociously.

The officer ignores the smile I can't prevent, or hide, as I'm making out their words. They come to me in a breathtaking unison and if I wasn't in cuffs, I would raise my hands now and join them, shouting at the top of my voice:

Action!

Now!

What used to be our slogan has become everyone's, but I'm still seeing you. I know it's our new We, making the waves of this sea, but I'm still hearing the words I didn't hear.

Do you believe me when I tell you that I'm saying them right back to you?

Look! I'm admitting to this, just the way you did. Please tell me that you still see me.

Do you still see me?

Five

Hope

The following evening, my flatmates and I are surrounding the feed in our kitchen. All three of us are hugging warm cups of camomile tea, the day's fifth or sixth round. My outspoken flatmate, opposite me, is wearing light blue jeans and a jumper that features the name of her university. Her quiet counterpart – next to me, with her chair turned the wrong way round – never bothered to get out of her pyjamas.

She woke me, with sparkles in her eyes, at six. I had fallen asleep five hours earlier, with my laptop still on my lap.

She helped me out of my sweat-soaked top and into a knitted jumper that's too warm for April but turned out to be the loosest piece of clothing I own. We both decided that there was no need for a bra, and that my black leggings would be just fine as trousers for now.

No shower for three days, the doctor said, but I had a careful wash. She came to the police station within an hour. My shoulder is very badly bruised and swollen, but not broken. I caught myself with my hands pretty well, she said. It's instinctive, apparently. She put the arm into a sling nevertheless, and gave me a painkiller prescription, just in case.

When she left the station, I still wasn't sure whether she believed what I told her had happened really had. Maybe because I wasn't so sure myself.

I'm being charged with intentionally breaking a police line and disobeying police orders, but the officers that dealt with me in the station were exceptionally nice. Once they agreed, shortly after midnight, to release me on bail until a court would reach a verdict, I was allowed to walk home – provided I would stay away from any demonstration or gathering, which, yesterday night, wasn't an easy trick to pull off.

A few hours ago, the official figure confirmed yesterday as the biggest mass demonstration around here in decades. And that was just this city; that was just yesterday.

I'm looking at my phone. My text messages to our ex-leader have grown more and more explicit as the day has progressed – but there is still no answer. And I'm worried. Despite all my conflicted feelings towards her, I need to know what she's making of what we're seeing, I feel; where she is right now; that she is... okay.

It didn't end where it could have ended. My quiet flatmate keeps clicking our laptop to refresh *#solidarity*. By now, there is no need to say for what anymore.

Things are kicking off here now too. Several central streets are blocked by people.

We haven't left the feed unattended for longer than fifteen minutes at a time. At first we thought: a near-by country. Then we thought: a few near-by countries. Then, time zone's were being bridged, continental borders no longer mattered. The crowds became bigger, the locations more unlikely. The list of cities grew and grew. Lunch was frozen pizza; dinner was frozen pizza too.

I look down. The tea that's left in my mug lets me see all the way to the white bottom, but my flatmates don't allow me to drift where I want – and don't want – to drift...

"Check that picture. What are the banners saying, you think?"

"How should I know?"

My outspoken flatmate shrugs. They look at me, but I don't respond.

We're looking at yet another country where the people were supposed to have other issues, more pressing concerns. Where what we're fighting for was meant to be an obstacle, a pesky hindrance: unwanted. Or so we were told – only by whom? Because those that should know best are clearly telling us something else, right there:

Action!

Now!

The people we've been seeing all day didn't have much, or anything, in common in terms of their languages, their religions, their cultures or their economic realities; what they did have in common was that look on their faces – and you didn't have to speak anyone's language to be able to read what it was saying.

"I still can't believe it. All this. Just because of what happened inside one parliament in one country, right? Isn't it amazing?"

I can feel my quiet flatmate's eyes on me, but I keep staring into my mug. I'm slowly moving it with both my hands now. Making waves.

"I don't get it. You're so quiet."

Trespass or terrorism – they still haven't decided. He could be lying in my arms tomorrow, or he could be gone for a very long time. The announcement is due any moment now. My flatmate keeps looking:

"I mean, what are *you* thinking about all this?"

2

This is what our walking looks like – that's what I'm thinking. And its almost too beautiful to be true.

I'm thinking: We're taking our first step out there, and no one can pretend not to see; no one can pretend not to hear our new We.

I'm thinking far too much. Out there, we're saying: Yes, we are prepared to shoulder some of the pain – to cut back our demands, to adjust our needs, to live a little differently – because the reward is worth it. Out there, we're saying: We are prepared to change!

And they're taking note. Almost all of them.

You may not agree with their tactics (and we don't), one staunchly conservative newspaper wrote today, but this country's politicians will ignore the message that's being sent at their own peril. So will we.

Had anyone told me on our café table yesterday morning that they would be writing like this, I would have spouted my coffee all over them. Yeah, right. I mean, them! Like this. What's next?

It's the right question to ask today.

In bed last night, I watched them over and over again. I couldn't get enough. Again and again, I looked at how they put away their scripts, re-arranged their ties, and started speaking from a different script, their own conscience. I have never seen anything like it.

This is what the brain meant, back in the bare room, when he told me about journalists going against the wave. Only that this is even better: Yesterday, I think, the wave itself changed its direction. And not without consequences:

Energy CEO speaks openly about a radical new business model. Can he mean it?

Mere tinges, of course. And yet:

Who else has read this? A group of appliance makers advocating self-imposed efficiency standards?

Reading between the lines of what companies have been saying today, breaking the Sunday peace with their unexpected press releases, statements and posts, I couldn't help feeling that something untouchable was being touched, if only very, very carefully – a habit?

I can't stop imagining the brain's face when he will finally see this. How many times has he repeated this mantra to us?

People, he used to say, as long as companies continue to use jobs, growth and competitiveness as a perfectly legitimate tool for blackmail to prevent any kind of change, we don't stand a chance.

I know that the brain would put everything that has been coming through today under intense scrutiny, but even he would be hard-pressed to deny that there's a certain potential in the air. If companies are really signalling, however carefully, that they might be prepared to voluntarily drop the tool, then I can't help wondering:

Are they beginning their walk too?

As for the government: If you forget the appalling initial response I saw on TV inside the police station, and the brutality they must have used to remove the two of them so speedily, and their denial, for hours, that anything significant had happened at all, then... I don't know. Aren't the words that have started to come from a few dozen line-breakers a sign that a foot is being raised, at least?

Some of the women and men I saw on my screen yesterday seem to have found what I wished they would find: their voices. Will they keep using them?

I haven't told any of this to my flatmates yet, because it's still so raw and unstructured, but I'm thinking: If we hold up our encouragement, and if companies bring on theirs, are these politicians going to put that foot down with real determination? Pushing us and companies further still.

Are we beginning to understand? The new We – that's the three of us, together.

I'm thinking: What seemed indestructible wasn't; the thick and clotted crust that cocooned the way forward until yesterday has been cracked, and it was cracked by the most beautiful wedge I could possibly imagine.

You.

3

Out of courtesy, I think, they haven't mentioned you all day. Even my outspoken flatmate restrained herself, I felt, swallowing her words on more than one occasion, unsure how to deal with the situation. With me.

But they've opened our liquor cabinet now, which currently consists of half a bottle of vodka, a red wine of unknown origin, and a label-free something in a sticky bottle none of us has been brave enough to try.

"So what about... I mean, what if the government decides that... you know?"

Make it a strong one, my quiet flatmate insisted. All day, she's been going on about how electrified she still feels. How it's as though she's part of something for the first time in her life. How her heart is still beating a little faster.

I wanted to tell her that I know exactly what it's like, and that, thanks to them, the issue is happening on a whole new level for me too, more beautifully connected than ever before – but there are too many other thoughts in my head.

I answer her half-baked question with a half-baked shrug and take another look at my phone. There's still no message from our ex-leader.

"You sure you don't want a vodka too? I'll mix you one. Come on. Let's celebrate you."

"I'm not the one who should be celebrated."

"Why not? Your picture is everywhere too."

"I really wish it wasn't. There's only one picture that counts, and that's the two of them."

They both nod. A young political assistant with a promising career ahead of him and a highly intelligent researcher with even better prospects, prepared to lose everything? For all of us.

Within twenty-four hours, the two of them have become the movement's defining image, a perfect visualisation of our situation. Iconic.

I zoomed in on the brain's face for the first time in bed last night. That's when I realised it was gone. The tension that had been threatening to tear him apart had vanished, completely.

Of course, I don't know how he took his decision – whether he was persuaded, or inspired, or whether he was much more of a leading force than I'm assuming now – but at some point in that process he must have realised that brave action for all of us might not stand in contradiction to his parents' expectations the way he had always thought it would.

The moment this sentence ran through my head I called my own parents. Right there. In the middle of the night.

I couldn't believe my ears when I heard – before I even said much at all – that my dad understood. In fact, he said, he had been thinking about the issue for some time now, and it wasn't too bad at all, probably, for things to be shaken up like this. Oh and while I was on the phone, I should talk to my mum, who just the other day had wondered if it wouldn't be nice to do something again, together, because mismatching lifestyles, long distances and prolonged silences shouldn't be in the way of what really counts.

The curtain collapsed, right there, in my bed; I couldn't believe it. I still can't.

The shot my flatmates means shows me, crossing the emptiness of the zone, framed by the parliament on top, and the crowd at the bottom. It must have been taken from a helicopter.

In the top right corner of the picture, you can just about make out the brain, as he's being carried away. The picture was taken before I noticed... You.

I look at the feed. What are they waiting for?

I close my eyes for what I've been holding on to, but the sound of my phone rips my lids the other way, and my initial feeling of relief – seeing her name, seeing that she's alive – withers as I read three short sentences that sound nothing like our ex-leader at all.

My reply is sent out so fast I can neither regret nor even just consider it:

"Let's meet straight away. I know a place."

4

A few minutes later, the city I have settled in, at least for the foreseeable future, passes in neon.

I close my eyes. I'm doing it again now: I'm taking our joint fight-back and I'm placing it at the heart of what we do.

Am I really daring to do this? I'm taking our new We – all three of us, walking towards each other – and I'm making *that* the core from which everything flows.

This is far too fresh to be written down. This is far too raw, but if we're doing what I'm doing, could we end up adjusting our chosen regime, almost accidentally?

I'm only just understanding this myself, but if we really manage to put our new We where I'm putting it right now, could we end up adjusting our chosen regime so it starts, once again, to serve those it was always meant to serve?

And, in doing so, dissolves? I'm smiling. Making way for what should really govern our lives.

5

"I slept with him."

"I know you did."

"What?"

We didn't say a word, walking up here. Not even hello. Not even how are you.

The shy hug she gave me at the hill's bottom was careful not just because of my sling.

She seemed unsure, though not about what she wanted out of it; she only stepped back when I turned my head, wordlessly, to point at the pathway.

She looks even paler than usual, worse than expected. Her curls are bound together in a tame tail, her legs pressed together, her hands folded, prayer-style, her shoulders slumped inside her jeans jacket. She is rocking, absently, back and forth.

"It might not seem like that all the time, but he's actually a very honest man."

"Right. Shit. I see."

I look at her, but she looks ahead.

Rocking.

It's a clear night. Our reds, oranges and whites are sharp against the black. The air, still unusually warm for this time, carries the city's sounds through the tiny holes of my knitted jumper, tickling my skin. She turns to me:

"So... what else did he tell you?"

"Nothing, I just..."

"Assumed he sensed a chance and took it? Fair enough. Sadly that's not what happened."

"No?"

I stare at her, but she's looking at her folded hands, less prayer now than convulsion.

"What *did* happen?"

"You know, when the blockades failed, something inside of me died... I... Fuck."

I would find her pause infuriating, if it wasn't for the pain I just heard in her voice.

"I was suddenly convinced that we would never win this. Given all that's working against us. But I couldn't get myself to admit this to any of you. I was so embarrassed. I mean, you all saw me as a kind of leader figure, didn't you? Even though I never asked for it. And yet, there I was, faltering."

"So?"

"I was so alone, and it's not something I'm used to. Maybe that was another reason for starting the group in the first place. Anyway. He came to mind. You know, I just wanted to go for a drink, or something? Have a chat?"

"Quite a chat, yes."

"He said why not and, I mean, why not indeed. It was so good to talk to someone again, about the issue, and about all sorts of things. And, I mean, the way he's holding up a conversation –"

"Let's come to the point."

"The more we talked the more I dreaded falling back into my depression, so I asked him if he fancied coming over to mine for one last drink, but he said that wasn't a good idea, and I can tell you it was in his eyes, then already."

"What was?"

"You were. I should have stopped right there, but I saw this emptiness in front of me, this terrible hole I would fall into if I would be alone again, so I kept pressing him and eventually he agreed and one drink became three simply because we kept talking so much, because we're both so... interested and have strong opinions, and there was definitely some kind of sexual energy building between us, but he would never have acted on it, but... I did."

Pillars are moving, ceilings rise; the entire construct starts to look different already.

"We were sitting quite close by then, and at the first best opportunity, I started to kiss him and he was withdrawing – I would be fucking lying to pretend otherwise – but I kept kissing him, probably in the most seductive way I've ever kissed a man, and, well, you know what can happen when you cross that threshold, and the defences collapse, and that's when he gave, just a tiny little bit, and that's what I grabbed."

But I don't see them anymore. I don't see her anymore. All I see is him, with me in his eyes.

"And then... fuck, he let a few things slip that night he shouldn't have. Looking back, it was all there, actually. What happened yesterday, I mean. The breathtaking, mind-blowing, unbelievably beautiful thing that happened yesterday. Anyway, he didn't want you to know. He didn't want you to be upset, he said. He was absolutely convinced they would emerge from this winning. He didn't want you to know anything beforehand, and worry."

"Is that what he said?"

"That's what he said exactly, and you should have seen his eyes when he did. I promised not to say anything. To you or anyone. But: One condition, I told him."

"That he wouldn't tell me how it happened."

Doubt, when attacked like this, bursts like a balloon, leaving nothing but a shrivelled clot. To be discarded at the next opportunity. Whatever was still in the way – it's gone.

"I was just so ashamed. I thought that if you hear it from him it might come across the wrong way and you might hate me forever. That doesn't mean that you won't hate me forever now, of course. All I can say is... how fucking sorry I am."

"Look at me."

It's the first time our eyes meet properly and everything she has said is still in them: I would not have believed anyone telling me that these eyes could look that vulnerable.

"Things might have turned out differently had I known some of this. But you could say that about pretty much everything. And, what can I say: I can see why you did what you did. In fact, I couldn't promise you I would have acted differently in your position. We're all just humans, right?"

She nods.

"Besides, you might have done me a favour actually. That's a bit hard to explain, though. Anyway, let's forget about it, okay?"

I was prepared for a grateful smile, a gesture of appreciation; I wasn't prepared for this: Her face has morphed into a smile that's almost what it used to be, and I wasn't prepared, either, for how happy that would make me.

She loosens her hands:

"There's one last thing."

"Yes?"

"God, I really hope this doesn't come across the wrong way now, but I think he's a wonderful man. And you would make a wonderful couple. That's what I wanted to say."

My mind is clinging to the *would*, but my heart grabs the *couple* and runs, leading my brown towards his green, and merged like that, our eyes make a colour I long for more than I ever longed for anything in this world...

Long minutes pass.

Over there, the tree rises in silence. Is it just me, or does it look weirdly unperturbed? Almost a little distant. Its dark branches seem to be swaying on regardless: As though nothing had happened at all. I almost laugh out loud at that thought.

Back home, it must have happened without me noticing: The blossoms are very unobtrusive, almost the same colour as the branches, a brownish orange or an orangey brown, and quite small. Here and there, I could make out a touch of green earlier. It all feels very understated, quite mature in a way.

It's as though my tree has waited out all the frantic activities of the last weeks, all those small trees rushing into a bud bonanza everywhere, whites topping pinks topping greens, everything springing, relentlessly, as though it were a race – to quietly come into its own as, elsewhere, the ripples are flattening. My tree, it seems, is doing things her way, and I'm loving it. *You would make a wonderful couple.*

When I return, her face is illuminated by the fake light of her phone.

"What is it?"

"Nothing."

The fake light doesn't conceal her lie.

"I mean…"

She places the phone on the bench in between us, so I can see for myself, but I keep looking ahead.

Everything that has been upset inside of me has started to settle down and it's happening throughout my body, everywhere at once. I keep looking ahead.

"Have you spoken to any of the others yet?"

"I only wanted to speak to you."

"Really, why?"

"Because I have most respect for you?"

"I thought the opposite was true to be honest."

"That means I'm even worse at showing some feelings than I thought I was. Did you ever wonder why I brought you into the group?"

"No, it just… I don't know."

"At first, it was just the brain and me. Meeting in a café after work. It was a joke, really, to have meetings in the room, but when the brain brought along that hipster girl he had met at a party, we just sort of did. Shortly afterwards I found a note in the room. From the ex-banker. Could he join whatever we were doing in there? I could never make sense of it, really –"

"Looks like he's as good at spying on people as he is at misleading them."

"What? I thought he was only there for the adrenaline kick he's missing from his job, but then he became such an integral part of us. I mean, he really did believe that it's ridiculous for the financial industry to be at the top of our system, dictating everything. That it should be the other way round."

He was there for the kick of love, but there's no need to explain this to her right now.

If the fashionista's text is anything to go by, the ex-banker is closer than he might ever have dreamt of becoming: There's something beneath the surface we're all seeing of him, she wrote. That's what

I've started to see, honey. That's what I want to get to know better, you know?

They are probably lying next to each other in his bed right now, her arms around his white chest, his hands stroking her dark black hair, their noses touching.

"How did you meet the brain?"

"On a conference I had smuggled myself into with a faked invitation. I was just getting active then."

"Why did you? Get active, I mean. I always wanted to ask you. Was it... your dad?"

"My dad? God, no. Did I ever tell you about him? I thought I hadn't. He's got nothing to do with it. Did you really think I was that one-dimensional?"

"Well, I –"

"Nothing can ever bring him back, and I'm not trying. That would be ridiculous. Sure, if we turn this around, people are less likely to die the way he died, but there are still plenty of ways to die, right? No... It was my belief that it had to be ordinary working people, fighting this. That this wasn't against us, but a hundred percent for us. About us. You know what I mean? And to be reliable in that statement, I figured, I had to place myself at the heart. Which is sort of what I tried with our group, but from the beginning I thought: Something is missing. Someone is."

She looks at me:

"That missing piece – that was you. And it fitted perfectly. I couldn't know it then, could I?"

There's still so much to be found, in all of us.

"Know what?"

"That you would also bring along the axe that would break us. Only to, well, look at what he's done. What they have done. I still can't believe it. Almost overnight, this has just, you know... exploded. Right into the centre. My biggest dream from the beginning! It's coming true right in front of my eyes. But it's so unfair that you have to suffer for it."

"Right, so how many years is it? I'm ready."

"I'm so sorry."

"How long?"

The prison I'm seeing is the prison I erected in my head this morning.

"Two years."

The walls of this prison are made of what looks like white froth or foam. Behind it, your silhouette is moving.

"Two years?"

She nods. I'm touching the wall now. Have you noticed me? I'm right here, with you.

"There are many men out there, aren't there? I mean, I wouldn't... I don't know."

I neither nod, nor do I shake my head at that; seen through the bubbles, your nose looks paler than it is. The moist strokes my hands as I reach out.

"But you're going to stay in this city, right? I really hope you will."

"Why wouldn't I?"

"Well, I don't know. I had the impression you were a bit... restless."

"Yes. I had that impression too."

It feels so familiar – your wet face beneath my hands, your uncovered arms around my waist. What difference do they make, the bubbles that are around us? What can they possibly be to us?

On this bench, our silence is now total except for our breathing, hers and mine.

I hear hers before I feel mine – steady, calm, in its own rhythm.

It takes me deeper, much deeper... But nothing announces itself, and I'm not surprised: Here, where they originated and descended, my attacks, things aren't raw the way they used to be. I don't know when it happened, or how, but fragility, it seems, has quietly undressed, revealing itself as something very different. Something very pure? The peeled result I feared for its vulnerability has started to show itself as something so precious I should feel privileged I'm in touch with it the way I am. My actual self?

And in front of you, there's no need to hide it. Sliding around my waist, your arms are pulling me against you.

"I need an honest answer from you. Don't worry about upsetting me, okay? But do you really think this can still go either way?"

"The government?"

"No – everything. That which doesn't have a name anymore. That which doesn't have a name yet. That which, maybe, doesn't even need a name. That."

"No."

"No?"

She's looking at me, but I linger on your lips. They're almost close enough now.

Slowly, I turn at her unsettled face:

"I think this is going to go the right way. But only if we all keep walking."

"Walking?"

"Yes, walking. I'll explain it to you another time, okay?"

"But please do, okay? Promise?"

"Promise."

"And so... so, you're going to stick with him, right? I mean, despite."

My smile is my answer.

I'm moving the finger of my sling-bound hand as though I'm playing the clarinet.

"Wow, isn't that, you know... quite a risk?"

I freeze them, stretched:

"And isn't that exactly what we've been talking about all these months?"

Your kiss, when it reaches me, makes everything else fall away. Whatever is beating inside of me and whatever is beating inside of you – they're so close now, there's no world left, but ours.

On our bench, she takes my unbound hand and places us in her lap.

"God, you're so right."

The tears I see on her – before I feel them myself – aren't the tears of despair, and they aren't the tears of sadness or the tears of loss. They aren't the tears of joy, either. I let my head sink against her shoulder. They are the tears of hope and she knows it and I know it too.

I feel her chin against my unkempt hair, her hand in mine. Her breath, from atop, covers me, like a light blanket, being placed in affection. I smile even though I know she can't see me. My fingers tighten around hers.

Over there, the tree's gentle swaying is more pronounced now, all its branches in a slow motion: For a moment, it looks as though our city is being carried in its mighty crown, our reds, oranges and whites cradled by its forgiving branches; at peace.

Soon, a pale rose will line these spires, blocks and cupolas. A dark blue dawn will gently push away the rooftops' black. Soon, a new sun will wake our city, and gently whisper at me, and gently whisper at you, and at her, and at them, that it's all down to where we take this, from here, but for now, all I want is to linger, like this, being held, beautifully still, by a little more than I'm used to.

I could tell you about what happened, of course. And I could tell you about everything that didn't happen. I could tell you about the prisoner that went on to become my husband and the devoted father of my daughter. And I could tell you about some of the best friends I ever had in my life. I wrote all this down, however – all those years ago – chiefly for myself. Re-reading my account the way I just did, I wanted to remember what it was like, in that special spring, when, suddenly, the speaking up for us and everything that surrounds us had become easier than it had ever been before. That's what I wanted to remember more than anything, I think: that beautiful brief moment in time when speaking up, even just a little, had the power to change the world forever.

Anna, November 2063

Thanks

Thank you, Omer Ali. Thank you, Will Atkins. Thank you,
Kathrin Anderl. Thank you, Brian Fitzgerald.

Your help and advice has been much appreciated.
Thank you all.

Christina – a sentence on a page like this can't express how deeply
grateful I am to you.

To you, dear reader – thank YOU.

About the Author

Daniel Kramb was born in 1982. He is the author of 'Dark Times'
and 'Three Lines Towards'.

www.danielkramb.com

www.ingramcontent.com/pod-product-compliance
Lightning Source LLC
Chambersburg PA
CBHW021016180626
46814CB00003B/1313